I0591052

Zombies and Cricket

Ima Ghoul

The Written Word Publishing

The Written Word Publishing

Australia

Email: keltoidrui@hotmail.com

https://wwwpublishing.wixsite.com/author

ISBN: (printed) 978-0-9756532-8-9 (ebook) 978-0-9756532-9-6

Copyright:

Cover design by YD La Marr

Contents

1. Chapter One: Nothing wrong with eight inches   1

2. Chapter Two: Green is my favourite colour   7

3. Chapter Three: Fair dinkum   13

4. Chapter Four: We can skip dessert   19

5. Chapter Five: Bird brain   23

6. Chapter Six: I still want us to keep our brains thanks   29

7. Chapter Seven: Home run   38

8. Chapter Eight: What good will that do?   44

9. Chapter Nine: An earful   48

10. Chapter Ten: It's snot a very good situation   55

11. Chapter Eleven: When the past bites you in the bum   67

12. Chapter Twelve: Going for green   72

13. Chapter Thirteen: A crawling hand named what now?   82

14. Different tropes for different folks   92

15. Alternate Ending One: Every dog has her day, even a zombie one   93

16. Epilogue One: Brain food   96

17. Alternate Ending Two: Brain smoothie   105

18. Epilogue Two: Green is still my favourite colour   109

Acknowledgements   113

About the author   114

19. Also by Ima Ghoul   116

Chapter One: Nothing wrong with eight inches

Gavin

I straighten my cricket cap and adjust my feet as I stare at the bowler, his green face devoid of emotion. The bowler glances down at the leatherbound sphere in his hand as if the act of remembering his task is too much. I puff out my chest, the circumference of that ball is just under nine inches, nothing wrong with eight inches; my girlfriend Alara hasn't complained.

Since the zombie apocalypse the world has had to adapt; while the inflicted are kept from rampaging with an adequate source of animal brains, the non-inflicted have had to change our lifestyles to incorporate their differences.

Our town is no utopia, but it's a mite better than what's happening elsewhere. It is October 31st 1982, the weekend, and like most small country towns, it is a day for local sports. It happens to be cricket season and my team, the Merinos, practice Sunday evenings. The remaining government has issued an equality clause where everyday the new populace and is less challenging, but I still enjoy the exercise and socialisation.

'Game,' shouts George after the second innings.

As we shake hands with the opposite team, our women rush forward with beer. I run a palm across my sweaty brow, doing little to relieve the hot stickiness. That beloved face greets me as the smaller, strawberry-haired woman almost dances restlessly on her feet. 'That was so exciting, Gavin.' She hands me a beer.

I crack the tin, the hiss reminding of refreshment as I scull the contents before crushing the receptacle in my wake. 'Not as exciting as before the event.'

The government, unwilling to accept an apocalypse, refers to the zombie invasion as The Event in all documents and forms of media. I draw my gorgeous girl towards me; her pale cheeks dotted with colour as I plant a steamy kiss on her startled lips. She lowers those innocent eyes to stare at her feet.

'People will see.'

'So be it.' I laugh, tilt her chin and kiss her again.

'Grrrrr.' A growl jolts me from my pleasant pastime.

As we separate, a green-skinned hand reaches for mine. 'Good match ... Grrr ... exciting.'

I shake Trudy's hand and grin as Alara blushes when her grandmother winks at her. 'Cute pair.'

William and George stride up to us and begin jostling me.

'Cut it out, lover boy, you will make us jealous.' William tosses me another beer.

'The team is meeting at the pub. The women are going to Moya's house for tea. The afflicted are excluded. So, there won't be many unafflicted women there. Heck.' George's eyes scan Alara's form. 'There aren't many non-zombie women anywhere.'

'I think I will just head to the library.' My girlfriend smiles fondly at me. 'I'm not great with people.'

Trudy clasps her granddaughter's arm. 'Best to go, love. I miss that kind of interaction, but the non-greenies seem to forget we were once their loved ones.'

Alara's eyes narrow on George and his gaze drops to her full, beautiful, kissable mouth. 'I won't go where my nan isn't welcome.'

George shrugs. 'Don't shoot the messenger.'

His gaze, lacking respect for another man's bird, makes me want to shoot the messenger. 'We don't go where greenies aren't welcome.'

The populace generally refers to zombiekind as greenies and the name has stuck.

The zombie bowler approaches us, his shambling steps belaying his condition. 'Urrrgh ... Good ... Grrr ... game.'

A woman next to him smiles in greeting. 'Nice to meet you; this is my hubby Robbie.' She clings to the zombie bowler's side.

I blink rapidly. 'Good game.'

'Grr ... un ... urgh sure was.' Robbie holds out a hand in sportsmanship.

George and William toss their empty cans at him

William spits at Robbie's feet. 'Fancy taking a non-greenie for yourself.'

'We were married ... arrgh ... before the event. We kept our vows ... grrr ... for in sickness and health,' says Robbie.

I step forward, take the outstretched hand and, not remembering my strength, shake it vigorously. 'Pleased to meet you.'

The poor man sighs as I draw away his hand clutched in my own. I swallow hard, his fingers squirm in mine as I hand it to his wife. 'Sorry mate.'

Robbie grins haphazardly as if his mouth doesn't quite shape properly. 'She'll be right, mate. My wife will reattach it later.'

That would be painful. Bile rises in my throat as I nod. 'Okay then.'

'We will be off then,' says Robbie's wife.

As the pair leave, I grip my girlfriend's hand before turning to my former friends. 'That wasn't okay. I don't think we can hang out anymore.' Then I stride away, Alara trotting beside me as her small feet struggle to keep time with my own.

Chapter Two: Green is my favourite colour

Alara

A s we leave the oval, we stop at the curb. The single traffic light changes as the little man flashes from green to red. How appropriate as a gaggle of zombies shamble across the road groaning, not at all unfamiliar to that of an employee moaning their woes on a Monday morning to their colleagues. The driver of the sole car stopped at the lights, plants their foot down. As the car zooms past, he yells at the gaggle. 'Bloody greenies again.'

Gavin releases my hand to press the crossing button. 'I'm at a loss. George and Will are supposed to be good blokes. I don't like how they treated that Robbie fellow.'

I smile up at my boyfriend. 'I know you don't. Just last week you carried an elderly zombie woman's allocated monthly portion of frozen brains back to her car when we went food shopping.' I squeeze his hand. 'You are a good man.'

My boyfriend's cheeks redden and he scratches the back of his head. 'Yeah, well, you got to help struggling people. Right thing to do. Sorry the match fell on your birthday and to boot you worked too.'

Being a notorious bookworm, my mind wanders and I become distracted trying to remember the name of the little figures in the lights. 'Ampelmännchen.'

Gavin gives me a bemused smile.

'Little traffic light men.' I point to the green man as we step off the curb. 'It's German.'

'Do you speak German?'

I shake my head. 'I read it somewhere.'

'I've got something planned.'

My stomach tightens with anticipation. 'You shouldn't have.'

'I wanted to.'

'Thank you.'

As we reach the other side a horrible guttural moan causes me to snap my head back the way we came.

'Arrrgh ... Grrr ... brains.' A zombie woman has stopped in the middle of the road; her yellow eyes roll back in her head before she rushes a man jaywalking.

The man screams and sprints towards us. 'The greenie wants my brains.'

As he hurtles towards me I back away and Gavin steps in front as the zombie woman leaps onto the back of the jaywalker, who crumples to the ground. He swats at her desperately as my boyfriend tries to pull the woman off the beleaguered victim.

My stomach plummets as the woman, dressed in pink hot pants, purple tie-dyed shirt and yellow platforms giving her an additional intimidating five inches over my tall boyfriend, slaps at Gavin with rainbow coloured two-inch nails. A streak of blood appears across Gavin's face. I rummage in my handbag and pull out a magazine and begin striking at the zombie. 'Back off, lady.'

The man cowering at my ankles crawls to the side and rushes to his feet and begins shouting. 'Help.'

Gavin stumbles up the curb and slips, careening with people on the footpath. 'Hey, shove off, mate.' A burly fellow pushes my boyfriend back towards the zombie. 'Not into watching couples fight.'

'I don't know this woman.' Gavin holds his attacker at bay, his arms outstretched. The zombie woman's wavy perm plastered with hairspray makes my nose wrinkle in the windy breeze.

I jump as blue and red flashing lights accompanied by a siren signal that the coppers have arrived. They pull up and an officer exits the vehicle and hurries towards the fray, his partner following in hot pursuit.

I rush towards the woman. 'Leave us alone.' My heart hammers in my chest, and I try to control my ragged breathing. This woman has obviously relapsed and is possibly stroppy due to not consuming enough brains. I know there's been a shortage lately and I hesitate. I don't want to hurt her if she can't control it.

'Urrrgh.' Gavin grumbles as the zombie's mouth latches on to his arm. 'Oi, you ratbag.' His fingers pry at her mouth.

The zombie unlatches her jaw, smacking her lips, her eyes close as if in reverence. 'He's tasty.'

'And taken.' Gavin covers the dripping wound with his other hand and takes a step back as a police officer drags his assailant away.

'Should get that looked at.' The officer nods in the direction as an ambulance pulls up, the lights flashing, the siren silent.

The other police officer hauls open the ambulance's doors as two ambos pull out a stretcher. The relapsed zombie is hoisted on to it, and she flails her arms and tries to kick the man holding down her legs. 'Grrr, let me go ... you tasty ... looking bugger ... brains.'

I stand there blinking in rapid succession, my breath halting in my lungs before I close the gap between Gavin and myself. 'Let me look.'

He gives me a broad grin and lifts the injured appendage to me. 'I'll be okay. Especially if you kiss it better.'

The zombie lets out a hideous snarl, and I turn to watch the macabre scene as an ambo opens a yellow bag, the smell of rotting meat and the intense situation hits me like a slap to the face. The woman now strapped down is force fed tiny brains, bile rises in my throat as my gaze snaps to that of Gavin's worried stare. 'No, not this. I don't want that for you.' I rub my arms as goosebumps form on the surface of the skin and I shiver despite the warmth.

The zombie woman quietens; her eyes widen and lock on mine. 'I bit your hubby, didn't I? Oh no, I am so sorry.' A sob catches in her throat and her yellow eyes are soon awash with tears.

An ambo hurries over to Gavin, removes his gloves and dons a new pair. His voice is muffled beneath his mask. 'May I take a look?'

Gavin holds up the injured arm. It appears deep; blood and green pus weeps from the wound. 'She got me good.'

The ambo peers into the wound and opens a first aid kit. 'I'll clean it and dress it for you ... but ... I am sorry.'

Gavin winces as the wound is cleaned and bandaged. His eyes betray his fear as he keeps a smile plastered on his lips. 'It will be okay. I reckon I'd look grouse in green.'

'I love you.' I begin to sob. 'Green is my favourite colour.'

Chapter Three: Fair dinkum

Gavin

A s I utter those words I know they aren't fair dinkum, but I'd do anything to comfort the beautiful woman whose heart is breaking in front of me. I sniff back my own tears as the ambo steps aside. I close the gap between me and my girl and haul her towards me in a firm hug. 'Hey, love, we will work it out. The pollies say they are getting closer to a cure every day.'

The man who cleaned my wound gives me a bemused smirk and begins packing up. 'I would get your things in order.'

He reaches into a pocket and holds up a pamphlet, my eyes scan the heading. Green and you, a guide to zombieism. I loosen my grip on Alara and snatch up the booklet and shove it into my jeans pocket. 'Ah thanks, I guess.'

'Bit of a doozy that you got bit on the anniversary of the apocalypse. Bit tongue in cheek calling it "Use your noggin day".' He lets out a lingering sigh. 'There's a number in there you can call for support.' He points to Alara whose head rests on my shoulder, her sobs still racking her tiny frame. 'If you think you are a danger to loved ones at any time, they can support her.' His face drains of colour. 'And they will deal with you.'

'Good to know.' I dip the brim of my cap to the ambo, turn and begin ambling towards the tractor parked nearby. My girlfriend clings to my arm.

'Wait,' the ambo calls out.

I turn as I hoist Alara up into the tractor. She opens the door and clambers in as the ambo hurries over and gives me a yellow bag with a picture of a green zombie face on it. I reach out and take the offering, the bag is frozen solid.

The ambo takes a step back. 'It accompanies the info. Keep it frozen until you feel the craving.'

'Oh blimey.'

The ambo smiles sadly before turning on his heel.

I shake my head and climb up into the cab of the tractor. My usual conveyance was once a Commodore, destroyed a year ago in an accident with a zombie roo. This would be unbelievable if it wasn't our actual reality.

My arm throbs and a nasty taste settles in my mouth as I lower myself into the driver's seat, turn the key and the engine roars to life. I feel Alara's warmth as she fidgets in the seat next to me. I place a hand on her thigh, the soft fabric of her knee-high skirt bunching under my big hand. 'I am sorry about your birthday, love.' A hand brushes my cheek and I hold it to my face. My voice breaks. 'Keep it there.'

As I change gears I have need of my hand, but hers still touches my cheek. My stomach churns and tears roll down my face, I glance in the mirror and her lower lip trembles. 'I'm okay, we're okay. I shouldn't be blabbing like a little kid.'

She lowers her eyes to stare at the mats on the floor. 'So, what do we do now?'

We reach the outskirts of town and I put my foot to the floor and we reach a whopping thirty kilometres an hour making the average twenty-minute trip to the farm in a car, a lot longer. I glance to the dash, the clock reads 7:15 and I feel like I've forgotten something in all the fuss from before. We've only been driving five minutes, but this journey feels like hell. Her hand trembles and I snatch it up and kiss it before dropping it gently and laugh. 'Your arm would be right sore if you left it there.'

She breathes long and deep. 'He's back.'

'Yeah, can't hold on to the bad for too long.' I stare ahead, the sun lowers in the sky; pink and gold streaks the horizon, the soothing sound of the aircon and the cool air blowing in my face calms my rattled nerves. A lone car passes us, headed towards town, and we fall into that easy silence that feels like home.

We turn into the yard and stop with the engine still running. I open the door and climb down to open the gate, Alara settles into the seat I had occupied as I puff my chest out with pride; I had taught her to drive the vehicle recently and she drives slowly through as I close the gate and parks the tractor nearby. Switching off the engine, the area, no longer lit up by the lights, settles into darkness like a welcoming friend. The night fills with the familiar chirp of crickets and the irritating hum of mozzies. I swat at one; my chest tightens as I lick my lips, trying to will away the intrusive thought, and now guilty pleasure, of wondering if mozzies have edible brains. So, the infection is spreading and relatively fast.

A feeling of unease settles upon me like it has frozen the blood in my veins. There is a low whistle, the sound of a bell.

A bleating ewe trots into view; a ribbon tied around her neck as someone turns the floodlight on the shed on. Alara turns to stare. I almost swear as I glance at my watch; 8:24. My best friend Murray and I had set up a surprise for my girl for her birthday when two weeks ago we had conveniently entered the jewellers, and she had glanced at me then the engagement rings with a wistful sigh. I had encouraged her to try on a couple, the next day I bought one of her favourites that had fit.

'Alara love, don't look. Now isn't the time.'

I rush towards her as she kneels to stare at the sheep, the words "marry me" sheared in its side and dyed in green, the colour she adores. I frown at the irony of it and what will soon happen to me. She bites her bottom lip while grabbing the box tied on by the ribbon.

'Alara, wait.' She opens it as I reach her, my arms drop to my side as I begin to shake.

What future can she have with a husband like me? She takes the ring, a small emerald set into a gold band, and slips it onto her finger. 'Yes, now and forever. No matter what happens.'

Murray steps out from behind the shed, pops two fingers into his mouth and whistles while Alara's zombie nan Trudy, scurries off the veranda from the shadows and claps politely.

'Congratulations.' Murray strides towards us and claps me on the back.

Trudy hugs her granddaughter. Alara stiffens, still not used to the affection from a once unaffectionate relative. 'Goodluck to you both.'

I hide my injured arm behind my back and smile politely. 'Yeah, great isn't it.'

Murray grins. 'I'll head back home now, I'm sure you two have a lot to discuss.'

'Can I bum a lift?' Trudy asks.

'Sure can.' Murray offers his arm and they trudge away from the house. 'It's grand they are tying the knot.'

'Sure is,' says Trudy, her voice carrying on the warm spring gust of air that teases the strawberry blonde hair of my new fiancée.

'Love ... are you okay?'

She glances up and steps towards me. 'Just kiss me, Gavin. We will manage whatever comes.'

'Strewth, I love you.' I lower my head and our mouths meet. A sense of unease clutches at my insides, like a terrible foreshadowing of death or the end of something so sweet I am not worthy enough to keep. As her warm lips touch mine it assures me I am still very much alive, for now.

Chapter Four: We can skip dessert

Alara

As my fiancé rattles around in the kitchen I sit blind-folded on the couch, tensing and untensing fingers before rubbing at my shoulder to ease the tension there.

'Let me.'

Warm, strong, calloused hands work their magic and my shoulders melt under his touch. The blindfold is removed and I glance up, his eyes glisten. 'Happy birthday, love.' Gavin tilts his head in the direction of the dining table. 'I'm not the best cook, but I made us a dinner even I'm proud of.'

I turn my head in the direction of his head tilt and my hands come up to cover my mouth, the well-worn wooden table is bedecked in finery like a lovestruck maiden at a ball; a shiny emerald tablecloth, golden silk napkins folded roughly into the shape of cat ears—one of my favourite animals—wine chilling in a steel bucket I know he uses to feed the chooks, and accompanying crystal glasses.

An old-fashioned, worn, white tin tureen, the flowers somewhat scratched off, his mother's treasured piece, makes my heart flutter. A setting for royalty and yet, still touches of my kind, salt of the earth guy.

Gavin gives a mock bow and, in that Australian country drawl, beckons me to be seated. 'My lady, dinner awaits.' He pulls out a chair and I glance at my stocky fellow stuffed into black jeans when he prefers blue, his work boots scrubbed to look almost new and his white singlet has been replaced with a white t-shirt. 'I wanted to scrub up nice for you.' He winks and runs a hand through his hair.

My eyes widen, he had cut his long, dusty blonde hair and I hadn't noticed in between the game and the incident. 'Oh, you look different,' I blurt out.

He laughs. 'Is that all?'

My cheeks heat as I stand. 'I like you both ways. And this'—I hold my arms wide—'is a magnificent gesture.' I stifle a sob as my heart fills with more love than I have ever felt for anyone. 'For someone like me.'

'I'll grow it back if you like.' Gavin frowns. 'You are my girl, my world. And most definitely enough.' He claps his hands together. 'Ice.' He hurries into the kitchen, the creak of the freezer door and soft thud as it closes draws my attention.

I break out into laughter as his brows narrow in bewilderment. He places the wooden tray with delicate carved handles that resemble feathers on the kitchen bench with indents for small bottles and a larger well for my quill. I practice calligraphy, a hobby I enjoy.

'I get it's a novelty ice cube tray, but how do you get the ice out of the little moulds?'

I stride over to him and wrap my arms around him. 'It's part of a calligraphy set.'

'Bugger.' He runs a hand through his short hair.

I smile. 'You really tried to think of everything.'

'Feel like a bit of a galah now.'

I draw back and he clears his throat and hurries over to the table and lifts the lid off the tureen. 'Made us some good tucker. Roast beef, with carrots, parsnips and razorback potatoes.'

My heart softens even more. 'Hasselback?'

'You must think I'm a bit silly.'

I shake my head. 'Not at all.' He takes up a carving knife and thinly slices the roast and places it on a plate, heaping the veggies and gravy on top as I sit down in a seat. He hands me the plate as I reach for the gravy boat and smother the meal in its contents before reaching for the salt shaker.

Gavin sits and does the same and we tuck into the hearty meal, both with an equally exuberant appetite. He smacks his lips. 'Happy birthday, sweetheart. I'm sorry I got bit.'

The atmosphere becomes stifling and I adjust the collar of my blue blouse. 'Great meal.' I smile, trying to defuse the situation while I shift in my seat.

'There's cake after.' He reaches for the wine and pops the cork, the rosé bubbles up and over the side and down his hand. He pours two glasses before sucking wine off his fingers and giving me a look filled with delightful promise. 'We can skip dessert.'

My stomach flops around like a fish out of water, and I blush, even after a year of exploring beyond my first kiss. I nod a little too vigorously and he stands up quickly, the chair screeching in protest as he sculls his drink.

He saunters over to me as I reach for my glass he takes it from my hand and lifts it to my mouth. 'Swallow.'

I know we shouldn't, not when he could change any minute, but this unassuming farmer has the seduction skills of Cassanova, and I melt every time. I swallow every last drop before he places the glass down and whispers the words he knows I love. 'Good girl.'

That's it, I swoon as he lifts me in his arms and carries me to the bedroom.

Chapter Five: Bird brain

Gavin

A lara snorts in her sleep as I sit on the edge of the bed staring at my hands. The brown digital alarm clock on the bedside table clacks over to 11 pm. I sigh and stand, hurrying over to the dusty window I should probably clean, and slump down into the recliner that has seen better days. I snatch up the pamphlet on the dresser I tossed there earlier, next to my lucky Akubra. Moonlight flickers across the skin on my left hand, now slightly tinged green, which shakes as I begin to read.

> *So, you are about to join the green team? It might seem grody, but not all is lost. We greenies can learn to control our ravenous desire for brains using the techniques of meditation, exercise and reflection. The changes can be swift for the more vulnerable, children and elderly turning quicker,*

and it is almost instantaneous. The longest to resist the disease was an athlete who held out for two days, but the symptoms are the same. First, you will experience strange thoughts and cravings for brains. Your skin will develop a green hue and your nails and teeth will lengthen and sharpen. At this point, you will need to chow down on brains daily to combat turning feral. Finally, you will turn completely green and your eyes will be a mustardy shade of yellow.

You should have received a week's supply of frozen pigeon brains to begin with. Consuming a larger brain too early leads to feralism, and pigeon brains are commonly available. Once the change is complete and a few weeks have passed, us greenies can manage on a larger brain per week.

For more support, join us at our meeting at your local town hall, held every Saturday in every town or city at 1 am. This is when there are less temptations about in case a greenie goes feral. Be wary, the likelihood of attacking a

loved one when you first change is very high.
For additional support, please call the Zom-
bies Ahh hotline on XXXX-XXXX.

I rise and pull a tank top over my head before slipping a pair of black shorts over my white briefs. I slap my hat on my head and cram my large feet into my boots with little care for socks, my chest tightening in knots.

Hurrying from the room, my boots thud softly on the wooden floor of the hallway. As I step across the linoleum of the kitchen the sound is muffled. I pull open the freezer door and tear open the yellow bag with my teeth, inside are seven plastic-wrapped parcels and I shove one into the pocket of my shorts as a horrible taste settles in my mouth, before I hurry back to my bedroom.

It seems my girl's not safe with me. I stride over to her and lift her in my arms, brushing a finger down her left forearm where I had accidentally grazed her with my lengthening nails.

She mumbles in her sleep and is the pinnacle of cuteness in her green pjs with a multitude of cats scampering across them. I wish my thoughts matched my bumbling words. She snuggles closer and is so small I can handle her in one arm as I reach for my rifle and hurry outside to the tractor. I lean the rifle against a huge wheel and kiss her awake. She wiggles her nose and I am tempted to kiss her again as her eyes flutter open and she slides down my torso to her feet.

'What is going on?' She turns to stare at the tractor.

'Not much. Get on up.'

Too sleepy to resist she hurries up the steps and fits herself into the passenger seat and closes her eyes. So trusting. I clamber up after and take my place. I start the ignition, the gears crunching under my hands as they shake. The thought to mung on her brilliant brain causes bile to rise in my throat. I feel for the tiny plastic-wrapped portion of offal; its presence is somewhat comforting yet makes me want to scream for the thought of what I'll become.

The scenery flows past, darkened trees, shining yellow eyes from the zombie roos lurking near the edge of the road. We arrive in town just after midnight as I took it a little easier, leery of the roos as one destroyed my beauty of a car last year that I can't afford to replace just yet. I doubt I will be able to drive in a few days anyway.

As I tun into Alara's driveway fear washes over me. Heck, I shouldn't even touch her anymore. Not being able to wrap my arms around her will be hell. My eyes nearly bulge and my heart hammers in my chest, the thought of being irresponsible and not wrapping something else causes me to gag and I thrust open the door and leap out to retch into Alara's sorry-looking flowerbeds. I really should get her home more often to tend her garden. I hurry over to a nearby tap and fill the cobwebbed watering can, the tap spluttering as water streams into the container. Stilling my trembling hands, I water her flowers. *It will be fine, we've forgotten a couple of times before and nothing happened.* I try to comfort myself. But this time I'm inflicted. How could I be so reckless?

I really am a bird brain. I groan, my hand instinctively reaching for the bulge in my shorts. Fitting. I hurry over to Alara's welcome mat to retrieve the key, inserting it into the lock and turn. The front door swings inwards.

I startle as Alara's hand slips into mine. 'Why are we here?'

I unhook our hands and gently push her inside, slipping the spare key into her hand. 'I can't, not now. I could hurt you.'

She looks up at me with wide, innocent eyes. 'Don't do this, please.'

'I have to.'

Tears well in her eyes and I am tempted to push her inside and carry her to her bedroom. 'Stay here for now.'

'But you asked me to marry you.'

My stomach clenches with hunger and I lift my hand to stroke her head. 'Strewth, love, this is already hard enough.' I turn on my heel and scramble up into the tractor.

'I love you,' she calls out, her voice trembling with intermittent sobs.

I look back and wave. 'There's always the blower, love. I'll call you tomorrow. Things are a bit different just for now. You are still my girl.'

The engine roars to life and I pull out of the long driveway. As I hurry towards the town hall my heart begins to shatter from the lie I so easily told. She is not safe with me until I can control these thoughts. As much as I want to her to be mine, I am lying to myself and Alara, that she is still my girl. I'll soon be hospitalised until I can control it. Then what? Will she be willing to wait for me?

As I park the tractor across three carparks lengthwise I sit gathering my thoughts. My mouth is dry as if I had gargled with ash. Hopefully this group can help me. First, I need a drink.

Chapter Six: I still want us to keep our brains thanks

Alara

A s the tractor roars away I scamper down the driveway like a frightened bunny, my tears streaming down my cheeks. I am tempted to run after it, my heart breaking when I roll my eyes and hurry to my own vehicle. Though we don't use it often, it is a great little car. A green sedan. I pat down my pajama top and realise my keys are at the farm and I grumble as I hurry inside.

Closing the door, I wander down the hallway to my room and with a click the room is flooded in warm yellow light. I begin to change out of my jammies into a black skirt and red blouse and shove the house key into the front pocket of my blouse before stuffing my feet into sandals. I need to figure out what his plans are.

I begin humming to myself, the catchy jingle that plays often during the adverts on the telly. The words replaying in my mind.

Remember, when you are feeling green and want to binge,

Use your brains and not theirs.

Make the call Arrrgh

Zombies Ahhhh, hotline on XXXX- XXXX.

I clap my hands together; of course. I hurry over to the rotary phone and begin dialling. I wonder if it's open 24 hours as I glance at the clock on the wall. 12:15 am.

The line connects.

'Arrrgh ... Zombies Ahhhh. How may I help you?'

'Ah.'

'Mamm ... grrr ... are you inflicted?'

'No, but Gavin is.'

'Who is Gavin? Brains.'

'My boyfriend, I mean fiancé. He got bitten and was given some information and brains. I don't know where he is?'

'Grrr. Do you have pen and paper?'

I nod then realise that is silly as the recipient of the phone call can't see that. 'Yes.'

'I'll give you the address for the group that should be meeting in forty-five minutes. They should be able to help

... grrr ... you. What is your city or town called ... brains ... please?'

I tremble as I whisper the name. I'll be alone with unpredictable zombies if Gavin isn't there.

'Mam, did you write down the address?'

'Oh right, yes, I got it. Thank you.'

'Is that all, Mam ... argghh ...?'

'Yeah, thanks. Bye.' I drop the receiver into its cradle and pull open the front door. Snatching the key from the lock, I tug the door shut behind me. So, they meet at the town hall. That's a twenty-minute walk from here. I hurry down the footpath to see my neighbour watering his garden. Zombies don't enjoy the sunlight and most seem to stay inside until evening. He waves; a sea-green afflicted Pomeranian yaps around his knees. 'I see you got Scamp back.'

'Grrr. Hey ... Alara. Nice night.'

'Yeah. How are you, Mr Aldridge?' I smile.

'Could be worse, you know. Steady supply of brr ... ains.'

'Okay, night.' I hurry past. I am not frightened of my kindly neighbour, but his zombie appearance reminds me if I don't get to Gavin soon he could go feral and be beyond help. I am tempted to run and break out into a jog.

Turning down the end of my street, I hasten along another before I rush across the road. I glance at my watch; 12:30. As I pass a pub, the patrons are stumbling out onto the street just after closing time.

Two of the men lock eyes with me and dash across the road and stop me.

'Hey Alara, why the hurry?' William's brow furrows. 'Where did Gavin get off to?'

My lower lip quivers and George's gaze drops to my mouth. 'Yeah. Why is his girl out here alone this late?'

A feel of unease prickles along my skin, settling in my stomach like a trap door spider ready to spring out and snatch up its prey. 'No reason,' I mumble.

'Gavin would be pretty upset if we left you here stranded.' William smiles kindly.

My heart bursts. Always one to wear my emotions on my sleeve, I break out into sobs.

'Why are you out here alone?' William asks more urgently.

'He got bit.' I shuffle my feet. 'I'm trying to find him.'

George holds his hands wide. 'You are in luck. He left five minutes ago after having three beers, looked a little green around the gills though.'

'Shut up, George. Gavin got bit and he didn't think to tell us.'

George frowns. 'Bet he's spewing about that.'

'I don't have time for this. Did he go in the direction of the town hall?' I glance ahead, before my eyes flick back to the men in front of me.

'Yeah love, he did.' William smiles. 'Goodluck.'

'Are we just leaving her to go by herself?' George scowls.

'Yeah, I'm not dealing with a bunch of brain-munching greenies.' William turns and heads to a nearby car. 'See you round.'

'Coward.' George shakes his head and reaches for my hand. 'I'll go with you, if you want.'

I snatch my hand back and his eyes narrow. 'Fine, suit yourself.'

I take a shaky breath. 'I'd appreciate it.'

We hurry down the main road and turn left.

'You know, if you want to give the zombie boyfriend the flick, I'm single.' George winks.

I clench my left fist, tempted to swing it in his direction. 'No thanks, I'm kind of worried about Gavin at the moment.'

The silence is suddenly deafening, the single streetlight flashes green as William pulls away from the curb and turns right. Screeching brakes cause me to turn and look as the car halts in the middle of the road and William rolls down the window and gestures to us. 'Listen to this. It's on repeat.'

George and I hurry towards the vehicle as William fiddles with a dial and the once-muted voice now blares from the radio.

> 'This is the national emergency line. Stay in your homes. Lock all doors and windows and gather emergency supplies. The infection has mutated and is now spread by scratch as well as bites. Authorities are doing all they can to prevent the spread. We repeat this is the national ...'

William switches off the radio as George pulls open the door and attempts to shove me in the car. I swat at him and he kicks my legs out from under me and drags me across the seat as he hops in.

'Alara's place is closer.' George sighs. 'Gavin's a top bloke and would want his girl safe. We are in the middle of an apocalypse and I'll look out for her.' He pats my knee and I push his hand off.

I had entertained my boyfriend's mates and William's wife and kids on two occasions. Once for Gavin's birthday and then at Easter. They know where I live and I scowl at George. 'I've got it from here.'

'I'll drop her off then we will go to mine,' William mutters to himself.

'No! I need to get to Gavin.' I fiddle with the door as the car starts to move. As it flings open, I roll on to the ground, skinning my knees and hands.

William shakes his head and slows down. 'I could have dropped you off there, love.'

George reaches over and pulls the door shut and William plants his foot. Their voices rise in unison in a chorus of curse words as they slam into a horde of rampaging zombies jogging down the street. One of the younger youth's has a boom box on their shoulder. The popular music is almost surreal as their golden eyes snap to mine, a long growl emanating from their almost slack jaw. 'Brains.'

I jolt to my feet, grit my teeth against the pain and bolt in the opposite direction. My sandals slap at my heels as I almost lose my footing with fifty metres to go. The town hall's floodlights come on as I enter the carpark and halt by the doors, my lungs aching, my breath spasming in my lungs. A small group of zombies and unafflicted are chatting in the entry hall, Gavin is amongst them.

'Shut the doors,' I manage to blurt out as I hurry inside.

The unafflicted turn as a dull cacophony of groans and roars reach us as the swarm sprawls into the carpark.

Gavin launches into action. He pushes me aside and slams the bulky clear doors shut and turns the key in the lock. 'What's happened, love?' His eyes snap to my arms as I hide my hands behind my back. 'You are injured.'

'It's now spread by scratches as well as bites. The radio mentioned it's out of hand and we should stay in our homes until the authorities contain the spread.' I drop my arms to my side. 'I was picked up by your mates and they wanted to drop me home. I refused and had an altercation with a moving vehicle and the road.' I grin.

'Why would you do that?' He snatches my hand and stares at it, brushing the bleeding, reddening skin with a finger. 'You'll do for now.'

'I needed to know you were okay.'

'I'm fine, love.' His brow furrows. 'But I need to get you out of here.'

'What about you?' I rush out, my breathing almost back to normal.

'Hardly matters now. You've probably got it too.' His eyes snap to the light scratch on my forearm. 'I haven't turned yet. I still want us to keep our brains thanks.' Gavin grabs my hand and hurries down a corridor, turns around the bend and rushes to the back entrance. He throws open the door, zombies are swarming near his tractor. Their heads turn towards us, their yellow eyes are wild, their tongues lick at their lips.

'Human.'

'Brains.'

'Grrrr.'

'Seems we are in a bit of a pickle.' Gavin pulls me into one of the meeting rooms and shoves a desk in front of the door before he leans against it. 'I don't know how to get you out of here.'

I gesture to the window. 'Plenty of those.'

He shakes his head and a slow grin spreads across his face then fades suddenly. He reaches into his pocket tears open a wrapper and crams something into his mouth.

'My brainy girl, better this than yours. He grits his teeth, his eyes filling with a hungry desperation like he either wants to eat me or kiss me.

Chapter Seven: Home run

Gavin

It is warm, chewy and foul. The smell is rancid and I almost gag. My stomach clenches and a sense of relief floods through my body. My brainy girl stands before me full of life as I am slowly losing mine. The thought to eat her crossed my mind when I went to compliment her for her cleverness.

'Get to the window then.' I grunt and push back as footsteps gather outside the room and shove at the door. 'Hurry.'

Alara scurries over and draws the curtains back, moon-light streams in through the window. She stands on a chair and unlatches the window. With a screech it slides open. Her gaze locks with mine.

'Go.'

'Not without you. We are in this together from the start, remember.' She puffs out her lovely chest in an attempt of bravery as her eyes glisten with tears.

I groan; my brave, stubborn fiancée. That word causes a wave of giddiness to sweep through me spurring me to action. Wife by morning. I'll make it happen. As if I could ever leave her.

She pulls herself over the sill as I run. The door crashes open and the horde tumbles through. A leg half over the ledge, Alara reaches down and begins flinging folders over my head. As a book lover I wonder if this will haunt her later and I grin.

'Don't worry, their filing system sucks. This brings me joy.'

There is a grunt behind me. I look over my shoulder, a zombie's mouth is inches from my elbow a folder stuck between the teeth in his dislodged jaw.

I skid to a halt and clamber up on to the shelves lining the windows as a zombie claws at my shirt and Alara slips outside. I toss aside the chair and pull myself up out of the window and drop to the ground as roars and groans gather and peak in the room behind us.

We jog across the local reserve, a growl and a green Pomeranian begins nipping at Alara's heels. She stops and the zombie dog stares up at her with adoration. 'Scamp, where is your owner?'

The dog barks and bolts before circling back. 'Scamp wants us to follow.' Alara leans down and pets the energetic animal. 'Who's a good girl?'

I chuckle to myself as Alara rights herself and gives me a puzzled stare. 'You certainly were last night.'

Her cheeks redden and she bites her lower lip. 'Shh, people could hear.'

The dog whines and scampers off with Alara in hot pursuit. We hurry down the main road and I halt in front of the sporting goods store. I pull off my shirt and wrap it around my fist and punch the window. As it shatters, I brush away the glass to slip my hand in and unlatch the door and push it open. I hurry inside and glance about, my eyes locking on the cricket bats and snatch up one before rushing outside.

The spunky little dog growls at a zombie woman zig zagging across the street, her arms outstretched towards Alara who squeals and ducks out of the way as I swing the bat. With a resounding crunch the woman's left leg snaps and falls to the ground.

'Grrr.' The zombie licks her lips, her eyes affixed on Alara's forehead before she stumbles and picks up her injured limb. I chuckle as the zombie leaves, hopping on her right foot just to stand behind a parked car and glare at me. Bloody heck, if looks could kill.

'My hero. Great home run.'

I wink. 'Wrong game.'

Scamp prances about then bounds down the footpath in the direction of Alara's house. The street is a post-apocalyptic hellscape. Zombies are burying their teeth into the unafflicted and afflicted, car alarms blare almost in tune with screams and growls, blue and red lights flash as the coppers and ambos are set upon. Small fires burn unchecked as a man with a can of fly spray and a lighter is burning everything in sight.

He turns to us; his eyes widen as they lock on mine. 'Back off, greenie.'

Alara steps in front of me as his hand shakes and the lighter clicks. I shove her aside and lift my bat, the smell of burning treated wood makes my nostrils flare. How dare he attempt to hurt an innocent woman. I drop my bat and lift my fist and punch him in the face. He stumbles to the side.

Alara grabs me around the middle as I pick up my bat. The urge to eat him surges through me. 'Gavin, your eyes are changing.'

I lower my weapon and give the man with the lighter an apologetic glance as my fiancée snatches my hand and sprints after the dog. We stumble amongst the debris of smashed glass and thrown objects; a half empty trolley rolls past. A group of teens are looting. Zombie youths and their affliction-free friends give each other high fives as if this is all some great game and not the end of civilisation as we know it.

We get clear of the chaos, running down her street towards her home. She stops as the little dog hurries in to the neighbour's yard and begins yapping. Alara follows and knocks on the door as an elderly greenie answers.

'Ah, there you are, Scamp.' His gaze settles on Alara's dishevelled hair and bleeding hands. 'You look a fright, love. Everything okay?'

Alara shakes her head. 'Your keys to your car, we need it.'

The neighbour stares at his car momentarily before smiling at Alara. 'Did you lock your keys in yours?'

'Mr Aldridge, here's not safe anymore and we need to get out of town.'

Mr Aldridge frowns. 'You sure, love?'

Alara nods and her neighbour hands her his keys.

'Do you have any family we can drop you off to?' I ask.

The elder smiles sadly. 'No, they have all passed. I trust in the almighty and I'll stay here.'

'Are you by any chance a priest?' My heart skips a beat.

'No. Just a retired judge.' The old man steps back as I stride towards him.

'Alara, want to get married now?' I grin. 'If it's the end of the world we may as well make the best of it.'

She looks at me as if I've lost my mind. 'We need to get out of here.'

'The judge can marry us on the way.' I laugh. 'Kidding, love.'

Chapter Eight: What good will that do?

Alara

I have never been spontaneous and if the end of the world isn't going to make me take a chance then nothing will. I stare up at Gavin, his gorgeous eyes are slowly turning a mustard yellow, but they still sparkle with that gentle love he offers me.

'Okay.' I reach for his hand. 'Let's do it.'

His brows rise slowly as if readying for take-off before he hugs me. 'Alright, love.'

Mr Aldridge looks at us as if we are aliens. It is so surreal considering he is a zombie.

'Ah the spontaneity of lovers rushing to the altar. Warms this old fellow's heart.' My neighbour hurries inside and we follow.

It is a veritable museum of doylies, dusty tomes, fraying wallpaper and other such vintage pieces. My neighbour hurries over to an ancient mahogany desk, and if it wasn't for the pens, I could imagine ink and quill as if he is a scribe from olden times. I giggle; like my set I keep at Gavin's. It would suit that desk so well and I could so easily envision myself as a lady from a different period and not this chaotic time when I could lose Gavin. I bite my tongue. No bad thoughts, Alara, get it together, I tell myself.

Mr Aldridge pulls open a desk and rummages inside and draws out some papers. 'I don't know how binding it will be. The news on the telly is sporadic and the reporters seem nervous, even in the cities.' He reaches for a pen and hands it to me. 'Fill these out.'

I read and begin filling in the application for marriage as the judge snatches up another pen and hands Gavin another sheet of paper. 'You too, young fella.'

The sound of scratching pen on paper is familiar and comforting as my nerves make me shake, threatening to make my teeth rattle around in my head.

My neighbour turns on the telly and images of chaos stream across the screen. A reporter stands away from a horde being pushed back by army personnel in combat gear, their guns barely holding back the horde whose eyes flicker in synchronisation to the raised weapons and back to the soldiers' heads.

'The government has temporarily lost control and the army has been called in to attempt to quell the masses,' cries the reporter.

'Not good,' Mr Aldridge mumbles as he takes our paperwork and scribbles his signature under ours. Pulling out a stamp, he opens a tin and dips it in the ink. 'Is there any reason why you two can't be wed?'

We both shake our heads. 'Do you Alara Anderson take Gavin Smith to be your wedded husband?'

My heart flutters in my chest like a frail bird. 'I do.'

'And you, young fellow. Do you take Alara Anderson as your wife?' My neighbour smiles.

'Bloody oath I do.' Gavin grins.

Mr Aldridge brings the stamp down on the paper. 'Congratulations, you two are officially wed. I'll file the paperwork tomorrow. But I don't know what good that will do. The authorities seem under a lot of pressure as late.' He smiles sadly and turns back to the tv.

Gavin leans down and kisses me as the news plays in the background.

'This just in. The cause of the virus has been located in a hidden lab during a raid. The company's name is Gentleheart Industries. A woman deemed as Patient Zero has just been freed, she is being kept in quarantine, but word has it she keeps asking for her daughter Grace.'

Gavin pulls back and his eyes widen, his head snapping to the television. 'No.'

I reach for his trembling hand. 'What is it?'

He pulls me into a crushing embrace. 'Do you remember me telling you how my first wife worked for Gentleheart Industries? And as you know, our daughter's name was Grace.'

My neighbour turns down the tv. The sound of my blood pumping chaotically through my arteries roars in my ears as sudden exhaustion floods my body.

'Alara, look at me. We can sort this out. It's probably a misunderstanding.'

'What good will that do?' I mutter as I pass out.

Chapter Nine: An earful

Gavin

My new wife slumps in my arms and my heart buckles under the pain I am feeling: love for Alara and the shocking news that Kelley may be alive. And what of Grace? All these years possibly separated from the family I adored, I thought dead.

A number flashes across the screen as the reporter rambles on about how they are hoping to talk to anyone with information regarding Patient Zero.

'I need a telephone.' I glance to Mr Aldridge who gestures to the one on the wall. 'Sorry, I'd rather have some privacy for this conversation. Have a good night.'

The judge waves me away with a smile. 'Enjoy your honeymoon.'

I pick up Alara and unfurl her clenched fist and snatch the car keys from her hand and hurry outside. I deposit my new wife in the unlocked car and dash to her house, unlocking her front door with the key I take from her blouse. While inside, I stuff a bag with clothes I have left there and some of my new wife's. Whatever happens, no one, and I mean no one, will take this woman from me. But I don't know if Alara will feel the same way. She's a real soppy sort and would sacrifice her happiness to see two forsaken lovers reunited. One of the reasons she stole my heart.

Won't happen on my watch, Alara is my bloody world. I grit my teeth before I sling the bag over my shoulder and pull the phone handle from its cradle and begin dialling. The line connects.

'Crime Blockers, how can we be of assistance?'

'Hello, my name is Gavin Smith. I used to be married to Kelley Smith who worked for Gentleheart Industries. Our daughter was Grace.'

'Please hold.'

I wait, wrapping the curly cord around my wrist while my stomach applies for a circus pulling off perfectly executed somersaults.

'Putting you through.'

The line reconnects. 'Hello Mr Smith. I am Mr Reed. I am investigating the case against Gentleheart Industries and I believe you may have some information in regards to Patient Zero.'

'Yes, I believe she may have been my wife.'

'I assure you she is alive. Well, as alive as a zombie can be.'

'And Grace?' My knees almost buckle.

'I would rather discuss this in person. Would you be able to visit us tomorrow?'

'Can't I come now?' I rush out.

'It's very late and Mrs Smith is very agitated.'

My mind centres on Alara. 'Can you stop calling her that, please?' I blurt out.

'That is her recorded name.'

'Please. I need to come now, before it's too late.'

'Alright, Mr Smith, we are situated at Hepswood Grove Hospital—'

'I know where it is.'

'Well, Mrs Sm ... I mean Patient Zero insisted on it.'

Where our daughter was born; my chest tightens. How much does she remember? 'Alright, I'm leaving now.'

'See you soon.'

The line goes dead and I slam the phone down and stumble outside. Pulling the door shut behind me, I jump over the garden bed into the neighbour's yard, and climb into the car. I insert the key; the engine of the large bulky ancient car roars to life. I turn on the headlights and back out of the driveway. As the houses recede behind us and we reach the open road, Alara stirs in the back seat.

'Where am I?'

I glance in the mirror; her eyes flit about.

'We are on our way to the hospital.'

'To get you help?'

'That would be nice.'

She frowns. 'I had a nasty dream.' She laughs nervously. 'That we got married and your wife was alive and then I passed out.'

I squirm in my seat and drum my hands on the steering wheel. 'Well, we are on the way to Hepswood Grove Hospital where my daughter was born.'

The large hospital covers the rural areas surrounding our town and I assume she knows of it.

Alara looses a long breath. 'Haven't been there since my parents died.'

I grit my teeth. 'Oh.'

'It's not far, is it?'

'Nope.' I slow down and turn left and pull up next to a 24-hour servo. As the engine dies, I open the door and slam it before pulling hers open and kneel before her, putting my head on her lap. Her hands stroke my hair. 'I need you. Kelley's apparently alive and a zombie.'

Her hand fists my hair. 'And you are taking me to see her?'

Doubt gnaws at my stomach and I imagine it chewing through the lining. 'No. I mean I hadn't thought that far ahead. I need to see her. Would you be willing to come with me even if it means you stay in the car?' Tears sting my eyes. 'I am asking too much of you.'

And this goodhearted, innocent, beautiful woman takes pity on me. 'Do you still want me near you? Your wife is alive. I don't want to come between your reunion.'

I pull away and her eyes are wet with tears; she sniffles and tries to hold them back.

'I swear to you on my life. Not that it matters much. Well, what I've got left.' I stare down at my left hand now a lime green. 'That after the past has been straightened out, you are my future. You are my wife. I have already grieved Kelley.'

I stand and pull her out of the car with me and draw her to my chest. She sobs and I rub her back. When she is finished she pulls away.

'Do you want anything?' I ask.

'Coffee.'

I nod and hurry towards the eatery. Several truckers have pulled up their semis nearby and as I enter the roadhouse that resembles a diner, several heads turn to me. I am met with the smell of overused cooking oil and burnt bacon.

A trucker cocks his head towards me. 'Loose greenie.'

A man flipping extra-crispy bacon on a griddle lifts his gaze to mine. 'What do you want?'

'Baby food,' I mutter.

He stares at me quizzically before pointing in the direction of shelves to the back of the store near the toilets. I hurry over and rummage amongst the dusty cans of baby food and snatch up the canned lamb brains. I hurry over to a counter with an ancient cash register and a woman pouring coffee.

'Is that all?' she asks.

'Two large black coffees please. Take away.'

She nods and as I hand over the money she counts out my change before placing the canned food in a paper bag and putting the takeaway cups in a cardboard holder. As I hurry towards the exit one of the truckers trips me and the bag crashes to the floor, cans go rolling to the accompaniment of laughter as some of the coffee scalds my hand. My stomach rumbles and I turn around, his shoulder looks tempting and I bite my tongue, my sharpening teeth slicing through the tender flesh, and I taste blood.

'Stupid thing to do. The blighter could probably rip your ear off,' says the cook.

I rush about, picking up the cans and tossing them in the bag all bar one before I place the bag and cup holder on the sticky well-worn floor. I pull back the tab on the can in my hand and lift it and its foul contents, cringing as I empty it into my mouth and chew. Bliss now lines my once temperamental stomach and I lock eyes with the man who tripped me. 'You're a nasty bugger. Lucky I'm only giving you an earful and not taking one.' I toss the can in an overfilling trashcan and retrieve my other purchases.

I turn and hurry outside, my boots making a tearing sound akin to ripping paper. They really need to clean this floor. When I reach the vehicle Alara has climbed into the front passenger seat, her knees curled to her chest. She turns as I slip inside, close my door and hand her the drinks. She gives me a weak smile and sips her coffee as I shove mine in the cup holder and put on my seatbelt. The rest of the journey takes ten minutes and, as we pull into the well-lit carpark, the sandstone building looms up like a daunting enemy, reminding me that this isn't the first hurdle in mine and Alara's relationship, but the first one as husband and wife.

Chapter Ten: It's snot a very good situation

Alara

I quell the urge to vomit, and breathe deeply as Gavin squeezes my shoulder for reassurance. We amble towards the hospital's double doors. I gulp as my eyes alight on the sign, *Hepswood Grove Hospital*. I haven't been here since my parents' deaths. I still miss them dreadfully and yet we are here as if the dead has been resurrected, not my dear mum and dad but Gavin's *real* wife, his legal and alive bride.

'You don't have to do this.'

Someone mutters something to me.

'My love, look at me.'

I lower my gaze to lock eyes with the man in front of me, his lip quivers and he chokes back a sob. 'Go back to the car. I'll see you soon.'

Gavin tosses me the keys, my hand flashes out and snatches at the air to catch them. 'I'm coming. You will need these later when we leave together.' That white lie is warranted if it soothes the tortured man in front of me, his eyes awash with anguish.

His jaw almost looks unhinged. I flinch, heck, one day soon it could do that. His frown turns into a half-smile drawing me away from my perturbed thoughts. 'You are one heck of a woman.' He absentmindedly pockets the keys I hand him.

Heat threatens to colour my cheeks scarlet and I hurry forward, pushing open a door as Gavin follows closely behind. We enter a wide waiting room with black plastic chairs too closely crammed together. An exasperated receptionist is tangled up unforgivingly between admitting new patients, answering calls and talking to the harried nursing staff. Gavin hurries up to the cream counter now enclosed by clear plastic with a thin slot at the bottom barely thick enough to push a paperback through.

The smell of harsh antiseptic barely covers the smell of sickness, a smell so hard to describe, but if I mentioned it to anyone they would get my meaning. I scan the room. A woman bounces a snotty toddler on her knee; the child's sickly mewing makes my heart soften towards the youngster. A man in the later stages of Zombieism moans and rocks in a chair, the surrounding area vacant of other patients. A burly copper on guard duty yawns. 'Stay clear of the area.' He points towards the counter. 'Best get on your way.'

Gavin snatches my hand and surges forward as if death is on his tail. Heck, it soon will be. Tears well in my eyes. *You are too dramatic.* I bite my lip and distance myself from the thought. 'You are an adventurer, dear Alara, here to accompany the ailing knight to reunite with his lost bride.'

The receptionist gives me a quizzical smile, shakes her head and motions my knight forward. 'G'day. What can I do for you?'

Gavin releases my hand and scratches his scalp. 'I'm Gavin Smith. I'm here about Patient Zero.'

The receptionist's eyes almost bug out of her head and she reaches for the handle of the phone, her eyes still trained on my love. She holds a conversation with the party on the other end as Gavin looks over his shoulder at me. I feel suddenly naked, as if all my problems and emotions are on display for him to pick over as he gives me an all-knowing look. 'You need to go take a seat.' With a sigh I shamble over to sit near the woman with the toddler. Her gaze snaps from Gavin's back to me as I suddenly straighten my form and give her a reassuring smile. The woman all but decompresses as the toddler gurgles.

As I slump down into the seat I twiddle with my thumbs until Gavin lowers himself into the chair next to me, his big form looking humorously squished. 'They will be along in a bit, Kelley's very agitated.'

'Oh my.' The woman across from us places her toddler in the pram and hurries past him. 'We will go elsewhere; we don't want you catching the greenie disease.'

Gavin's gaze fixates on the cheap, white plastic clock on the opposite wall. Time ticks by as if the world hasn't fallen to chaos and this is your average doctor's visit. His eyelids lower twenty minutes in and his soft familiar snores are almost comforting. Forty minutes later and I am tempted to join him; you would think with this new information the authorities would be hurrying to meet us.

Someone clears their throat and I bolt upright, fixing my skirt in the process before I prod Gavin with a finger who almost leaps out of his seat.

'I'm awake.' Gavin adjusts his hat and stares at the man dressed in a dapper two-piece striped suit.

'I am Trevor Reed. Are you Mr Smith?' Trevor holds out his hand.

Gavin shakes it. 'Yeah, just call me Gavin.'

'I understand this must be daunting news.' Trevor trains his gaze on mine and he frowns. 'Who is this?'

Gavin puffs out his chest, reminding me of a sassy cocky about to dance for his mate, and I squeeze my traitorous lips together, preventing the urge to smile.

'She's my wife and I want her to go with us.'

'I see.' Trevor turns on his heel and Gavin falls in line beside him. 'We have filled Mrs ... Kelley in on the fact you were told she was dead and how the company lied to you saying the body carried deadly pathogens and needed to be burnt and how it had to be done in an isolated setting.'

The men hurry down a corridor, I trail behind them. We take a left and hurry past a woman pushing a tea trolley; the wheels squeak and she gives us an almost apologetic smile.

Trevor halts before a steel door with a familiar logo, a green caricature of a zombie face on a yellow square, the words *Zombies ... Ahh* on the door makes me want to almost roll my eyes with the absurdity of the name.

Gavin gestures to the door with an enclosed fist, thumb sticking out. 'Ah, not very subtle hey.'

Trevor shrugs. 'At least you know to be wary.' He presses a button on a grey intercom.

With a buzz the line connects. 'Hello, welcome to Z ward, how may I be of assistance?'

'It's Trevor Reed from Crime Blockers. I am with a Mr Smith and ...' He glances back at me.

'Mrs Smith.' Gavin's eyes almost smoulder as they settle on my forehead. My husband licks his lips as if he's not sure whether to eat me or take me elsewhere for some alone time.

'And Mrs Smith to see Kelley Smith.' Reed releases the button.

'Okay, I'll buzz you in.' The intercom goes silent. A loud buzz grates on my nerves as the doors open outwards.

Trevor steps forward and we hurry after him as the doors close behind us. The new area is covered in clear plastic like a see-through tent, yellow caution signs litter the walls behind our cocoon. Trevor removes his suit jacket, placing it in on one of the grey vinyl benches, dons a yellow disposable apron and a white paper mask. He grabs an alcohol wipe from a dispenser, wipes his hands before tossing the contents into a black bin and pushing his rather small hands into thick, blue rubber gloves from a nearby alcove. 'They like to take a bite out of hands. When they turn, sometimes the faces of loved ones can set them off, so please cover up and refrain from bombarding her with too much information.'

Gavin nods and dresses. His shoulders slump and he glances at the caution signs and shudders.

I place a hand on his shoulder. 'I'm here for you.'

My husband reaches out, squeezes my hand with his large, calloused one before putting on his mask. I scramble to dress, the smell of alcohol and antiseptic makes my nose twitch. Trevor pushes the plastic drapes aside and hurries down a barren corridor, grey-speckled linoleum floors, white walls free of artwork except more yellow caution signs that are now grating on my nerves. We get it, there is danger in a zombie ward. A wave of hopelessness washes over me, my breath quickens as I stare at my husband's form. This is where he may end up. Heck, they all do before they can be released back into the outside world. A doctor in a white lab coat, clipboard clutched in his right hand, approaches us. My eyes flick to his name badge. Dr Dalage.

The doctor frowns his gaze sweeps over Gavin's form. 'Are you to be admitted?'

As Gavin nods my stomach drops.

'No, we are here to visit someone,' I blurt out.

'Alara.' My husband steps towards me. 'I am changing and this is the best place for me for now. I won't be able to hurt anyone.' His voice wavers, almost as if it will crack. 'I can't risk hurting you.'

I stumble over my next words, my heart competing in a rapid sprint. 'But my nan was fine.'

'After she was processed.' Gavin turns back to the doctor.

As the three men hurry down the hall they enter a small room with comfortable couches. Gavin begins reciting his identifying information as the doctor fills out a form, left handed I note.

I squash down my pain and try to smile, but I reckon it's more of a horrid grimace, a poor attempt at support. Gavin gets to see his beloved again. Heck, they are both zombies, their reunion will be even more poignant, two distraught souls lost at sea, their love a lifeboat in the hellish apocalypse sea.

I wander over to a counter boasting a large white urn, glass bowls filled with tea bags, tiny plastic milk containers, instant coffee and sugar sachets and those thin wooden stirrers.

I make myself a cuppa; the smell of strong tea and steam wafts over my cheeks as I lift the cup to my mouth. I needed that, it's amazing how such a simple ritual can soothe ragged nerves.

The doctor clicks his pen. 'Right, we will go see Mrs Smith and then we will see you settled.'

I scull my drink and toss the cup in a bin as all three men stand.

Dr Dalage gives me an apologetic smile. 'I am sorry Mr Smith, but your friend cannot accompany you. She is not a relative of Kelley who believes she is still married and ... I didn't catch her name.'

Gavin grumbles. 'Alara Smith, she is my legal wife.'

Dr Dalage's brow furrows. 'Well, your legal wife is still technically alive, so unfortunately, we cannot recognise

Miss Alara as your wife and she has no direct relation with your lawful spouse so will be not allowed to visit.'

My husband, soon-to-be someone else's, whips off his lucky hat and strides towards me. I cannot meet his questing, demanding gaze, and he drops the hat on my head. It smells of sweat and is warm from contact with his head. 'I'll be back for it.' He dips his head and tries to kiss me and I back away. 'You have a wife.'

Gavin's eyes darken. 'Yeah, you!'

He turns on his heel and strides out of the waiting room. Dr Dalage sighs and follows, as does Trevor. Once they have left, my knees buckle and I slide down against the counter and let the pent up feelings explode in a cascade of hot tears.

Gavin

Bloody stubborn, sappy woman. I hurry out of the waiting room and wait for Dr Dalage to catch up and lead the way. I bet she has some ridiculous notion that once I see Kelley it will awaken some great romantic feelings and I will forget my sweet, odd, little librarian, not a chance. I have grieved Kelley and, while I care that she is treated well, it's not the same as it was, I tell myself. I trail behind the doctor and Trevor. We make a few turns, enter an elevator and ride up another floor. As we step out the ward is pleasanter, pictures of forests, beaches and other soothing scenes litter the walls. Bunches of flowers in glass vases occupy various places such as a desk and a coffee table strewn with magazines and accompanied by comfy couches.

'This is the private ward for direct victims of Gentle-heart Industries.' Dr Dalage scowls. 'They donated a huge amount of money like it justifies what they did.'

I frown. 'What exactly happened?'

'Now that you've signed a confidentiality form I can tell you.' Trevor sighs. 'Gentleheart Industries had a side business, an offal processing factory. Their health foods and toiletries were failing so they allowed their scientists to experiment with restricted organisms. They came up with multiple serums and released it into their popular foods, unleashing catastrophic plagues around the world. Your wife took the first serum and that virus is spread through contact with body fluids, bites or scratches.'

The last few words fade into ringing in my ears and I lean a hand against the wall. 'You need to have Alara checked,' I choke out and turn back to the doctor. 'We did married things.'

Dr Dalage gestures to a nurse. 'Jessica, could you please go and escort Alara who is in waiting room A to my office.'

The nurse nods and hurries away.

Alara

I smile after the unleashing and sniffle. I reckon I look like that snotty toddler now. This is an awful situation and I see no happily ever after. *Come on, Alara, you are tough, you can get through.* My nose leaks and I stand up and snatch up a napkin and wipe it.

'Ha, it's snot a very good situation.'

The cheesy joke is lost on the nurse who approaches me. 'Alara?'

'Yes.'

'I am nurse Jessica. Doctor Dalage has asked me to accompany you to his office to wait for him.'

'Why?' I dig my fingernails into my palms.

'Well, Mr Smith said you have had intimate relations and we are not sure if it can spread the virus.'

My cheeks are set ablaze. 'Does everyone need to know that?'

The nurse turns on her heel with a tired sigh. 'Please follow me.'

Chapter Eleven: When the past bites you in the bum

Gavin

A s Trevor and the doctor halt outside Room C1, my gaze is locked on the identifying plaque. Dr Dalage knocks.

'Come in.' That once familiar voice which made my heart soar is like a dead weight wrapped around my ankles as I drown in a sea of guilt and fear. The doctor smiles and enters the room; I hold back for a moment, my hands fisted into the pockets of my jeans.

'How are you today, Mrs Smith?' Trevor enters the room.

It is a pleasant one to be sure, decorated in benevolent watercolours, a comfy couch, a door leading off to what I assume is an ensuite and a reasonable looking hospital bed.

Nestled amongst pillows and copious amounts of blanks sits a frail woman. Her yellow eyes lock on me and widen and she reaches out a hand. 'Gavin. Is it really you?'

I take a deep breath and sidle past the other occupants and take a seat on a rather uncomfortable plastic chair off to the left side of the bed and within reach of Kelley. 'They told me what happened.'

She smiles sadly. 'Oh, and how are you?'

I chuckle. 'In a similar situation it seems.'

'Can I have a moment alone with him? I am well enough to see him.' Kelley smiles at Trevor.

Trevor and the doctor excuse themselves and close the door behind them.

Tears well in Kelley's eyes. 'Grace is dead.'

I reach out and squeeze her hand, my heart explodes with reawakened grief and I choke out a reply. 'Yeah, I know ... I miss her too.'

'They say it's been over eight years.'

I nod. 'Been rough for me, but I reckon it was harder for you.'

She grips my hand harshly. 'They kept me locked up inside a room. Sometimes I got outside in the evenings. They took regular blood samples and, apart from that, left me to my grief. My only thought was to get back to you after Grace's death.'

I strangle the urge to scream. How could they do that to her? 'But you are okay, apart from the zombie stuff, right?'

She shakes her head. 'I have a lot of trauma to work through. But I have you now, so that's something.'

I loosen her grip and slide my hand away. 'Yeah, I really spat the dummy. At one point I didn't' want to be here. You will always be an old mate. I'll make sure you get plenty of tucker and a decent quack.' As those words leave my mouth I close my eyes, tears threatening to bust them open again. You are a callous bugger; here is your former wife all full of hope and love for you and you just tore it from her like an adhesive bandage ripped off arm hair.

'Grrrr.'

I open my eyes Kelley's face is distorted and she resembles a Tassie devil. 'Did you just growl?'

My ex tosses the blankets aside 'Who is ... grrr ... she?'

'We don't need to mention it. You should get some rest. I'll visit again soon if you like.'

And like the mighty stoic little marsupial, she leaps at me, the chair crashes to the floor and I snatch at her hands which tear at my clothes, her faces inches from mine.

My eyes widen as she presses her lips on mine. I drag my head away. 'Enough of that, love.'

'Where's your hat? You never took it off except when you slept, practiced cricket or showered?'

I glance away.

'You gave it to her, didn't you?'

I push her off me and she slides back on to her haunches looking weak and pitiful. I stand and lift her into my arms and place her back into the bed, drawing the covers up over her and turn away to right the chair. I yelp when something feels like it bit me on the bum through my jeans like a row of tiny needles.

I turn sharply; Kelley gives me a demented smile. 'Well, I left my mark on you. Explain that to her.'

'Did you just bite me on the bum?' I rub the offended area.

She breaks into demented laughter. 'Yeah. This is surreal, aint it?'

'Strewth, you're not half wrong.' I scratch my head.

'Who would have thought an evil corporation and zombies would tear us apart?' She stares at her hands. 'I am sorry for becoming this.'

Her desperate admission causes me to make a sound of despair and I lean over and place a hand on her shoulder. 'I did love you proper, you know.'

Her gaze softens. 'I'm a jealous cow, but I understand. You grieved and moved on because you thought I was dead. How long before you dated?

'We didn't date. Kind of fell into it, zombie apocalypse and all.'

She raised a brow. 'Oh, so recent. Do you love her?'

I nod, unable to find quite the right words when the woman you thought dead comes back as a zombie and declares their love for you and asks if you love another.

Kelley lets out a loud bloodcurdling growl, 'Grrr. Unghh ... Go be with her and forget me. I don't want to see you again!'

The door flings open and a nurse comes in, trying to soothe Kelley as I back out into the hallway. I lean my forehead against the cold, hard wall and unleash a fit of sobs of my own. Knowing Kelley as I do, she had acted that way to severe any marital connection between us and set me free from her and her own aching heart. My sense of duty says I should honour my vows to Kelley, but Alara now owns my heart. But how can I be with Alara when I am turning into a zombie?

I push my way back into the room. Kelley is sobbing in to a tissue, she lifts her eyes to mine and smiles. 'You've chosen me?'

Chapter Twelve: Going for green

Alara

This room is organised chaos; out of boredom I set myself to memorising it. Navy carpets, beige walls. Urgh, who was the interior decorator? Cream filing cabinets and a large austere walnut desk takes up most of the small room. I sigh and stare at the little decorative bird swaying back and forth slowly absorbing the contents of a tiny glass. I bypass the heavy stapler to spin the rolodex in front of me before picking up the phone and impersonating a receptionist, twirling the long, coiled cord in my other hand before replacing it back in the cradle.

I turn in my seat as Doctor Dalage enters his office and plops into a chair at the head of the desk opposite me. 'We have the results.'

I absentmindedly rub the area on my left arm taped with cotton wool where they took my blood an hour ago. 'And?'

'You have the virus.' He sighs. 'Could be minutes, hours or days before you change.'

I can be with him. I rub my shoulders as a feeling of relief washes over me before doubt creeps in like a niggle gremlin. He should choose Kelley, he loved her first.

'Now, I have some paperwork for you to complete before you can be admitted.' He opens a drawer and pulls out some papers and shuffles them before handing them over.

Gavin

I take a seat next to Kelley and she sits up and reaches down over the other side of the bed and pulls up a worn cricket bat. My heart stills momentarily as she places it across my lap. The white-wrapped handle is worn and dirty; I trace my hands along where my initials and her maiden ones are engraved in the face. 'They let you keep it?'

She smiles. 'They replaced the initial casket with a fake one before they cremated it.' Her lips tremble. 'It was dark in there. I witnessed what it was like to be entombed if only for a few minutes. They didn't think there was harm in leaving the bat with me.

I lean the bat against the bed. 'I can't accept this, Kel.'

She runs her fingers up my arm to rest on my hand. 'So, it's truly over then.'

Tears stream down my cheeks. 'I am so sorry. I feel bloody awful. But I can't lie to you, mate.'

She draws her hand away and sighs. 'Go be happy then. I release you.

'I don't want to part on painful terms, Kelley. I am admitted to this hospital until I can be processed and leave. I will sit with you sometimes so you have a familiar face nearby, but you must understand I want you in my life as a friend. But my wife is now Alara and I have to meet her in Doctor Dalage's office to see how she's doing.'

'Please don't forget I exist. Keep your promise to visit occasionally. I'd like to meet her at least once. It's probably for the best, you know, I never really followed cricket.'

I tilt my head. 'But we met at a match.'

She laughs. 'A friend dragged me there and I thought you were kind of rad.'

'Blimey.' I grin. 'Never figured you didn't like cricket.'

She pats my hand. 'After our first date I went to the library and this wonderful young librarian helped me research it.'

I chuckle. 'I'll forgive you.'

'The woman was very sweet and never got flustered when I kept the books too long.'

My heart skips a bit. 'Did she happen to have strawberry blonde hair?'

Kelley nods.

'Well, you've met Alara then. I'll have to ask if she's putting on her love of cricket too.' I rise up out of my chair and stretch. 'I will see you in a bit.'

The door creaks open as if someone had held it ajar and listened in. Susan, Kelley's old boss, stands in the doorway. I glance at my ex, her cheeks are ashen grey under the green hue, her eyes are wide with fear.

Three large men enter the room and surge towards me, I leap to my feet, pick up a water jug and hurl it at them before one unclips a gun from his holster and fires; the bullet stings as it embeds in my leg. I roar, spittle firing from my lips into the man's face as I grab his shirt and smash my fist into his head, there is a horrible crack and the man grabs his bleeding nose.

Susan gestures to another woman, I turn and stare at her mirror image. 'Meet one of my younger clones. Model S2.' She gestures to herself. 'I am S1.'

S1 reaches for a walkie talkie, it buzzes as she presses the talk button. 'Susan, there's another talker. Doctor

Dalage's office. A woman name Alara, assuming last name Smith.'

Like she had recorded herself talking, her voice answers from the speakers. 'Hear you loud and clear, S1. On our way.'

S1 advances on my ex. I sprint towards the two women dodging another of the thugs like a shearer avoiding an enraged ram, and tackle her from behind. As the woman slumps to the ground I throw myself to my feet.

Kelley gives me a weak smile. 'You've fully turned.'

I nod. 'Yeah, I can feel the strength bubbling to surface along with the horrid craving for brains.'

I stumble away from her, dragging S1 out of the room. The thugs follow me two steps behind. An alarm rings in my ears as a nurse flicks a switch. Red lights begin to flash and all I can think of is rescuing Alara and eating the nurse's brain. I fumble in my pocket for the last can of baby food, pull it out and stare at it. As a thug aims his gun at the nurse I toss the can at the gun. It dips to the left and fires, a bullet lodges in the wall near the frightened nurse.

Lunging forward, the man screams as I bite into his arm. 'Going for green,' I mutter as I latch on to his ear and hurl myself backwards, the thug screams and stares at his bloodied hands.

I turn and boot the other thug in the dingleberries and he groans and falls to his knees before the other aims his gun at Kelley. I back into the room, pretending to lower myself into the chair and reach for the bat. A scream tears from my body as Kelley clutches at her chest as a gun discharges.

'Crap. We were supposed to end them quietly, let's go.' S1 hurries from the room and slams into Trevor's chest.

'Arrest them.' Trevor straightens his jacket. 'This evil corporation must be brought to justice.'

A swarm of security guards, nurses and doctors enter, and I back up against the wall, the bat clutched in my hand.

'Go, Gavin. Go to her. Tell Dalage to enact my final wishes.' Kelley points to the door.

A machine beeps, voices yell and the urge to taste the contents of people's skulls fills me. 'I can't leave you like this, Kel.' My brain and sense of loyalty forces me to falter for a second.

'For what it's worth, you were worth it.' Kelley screams and her eyes close.

'Ditto, Kel,' I reply before my heart makes a decision and I push past the doctors, hurrying down the chaotic corridor swarming with medical staff. Doors crash open and angry patients begin to latch on to the poor staff.

I fling one zombie aside and lean down and help a distressed orderly to his feet. 'Doctor Dalage's office.'

The man points behind me. 'Follow to the end, turn right and third door on the left. You aren't going to eat me?'

'I kind of want to, but I have more pressing matters.'

The man gulps. 'Thanks, I guess.'

Security personnel flood into the space and start using brute force to wrestle the zombies away from the medical personnel. One spots me and hurries towards me. 'Back off, greenie.'

The orderly steps in front of me. 'He's with me.'

The security officer nods and returns to the fray.

'Thanks.'

The younger man smiles at me before hurrying away.

Alara

As I take the pen the doctor holds out there is a knock on the door.

Dr Dalage gives me an apologetic smile. 'Come in.'

His smile fades and his eyes widen. I look over my shoulder as a woman dressed in a black tailored suit enters the room followed by three burly guys dressed in white shirts and black trousers. One of the men slams the door shut and leans against it, my gaze locks on the gun holster on his hip.

Dr Dalage pushes back his seat and stands. 'Get out.'

The woman grins. 'Hush. We own this ward and have our own keys. We just checked in on our former employee. Seeing how much her tongue was wagging made us want to ask you a few questions.'

My stomach plummets like an elevator in free fall and I scramble out of my seat and face them. They better not have harmed Gavin and his lady love. I reach for the bird and grit my teeth. Dr Dalage shakes his head at me before he smiles disarmingly at the woman. 'Susan. What have you done with Mrs Smith?'

Susan reaches into her pocket and pulls out a small black case which she proceeds to unzip. She gestures to the man next to her who approaches the doctor and grabs his arms behind him in a vicelike grip. As the medical professional struggles, I lean against the desk and snatch up what I can find with a hand behind my back. Susan saunters towards us, pulling two syringes and a vial from the case. She tosses

the case aside and proceeds to unwrap the medical appa-
ratus and plunge them into the vial and draw up the thick
cloudy fluid.

'Mr Smith was all too eager to give up Alara's name
when we threatened Kelley's life.'

A sob begins in the hollow of my throat and rises upwards with the bile from my stomach and I cough, trying
to force the air into my lungs. *He chose Kelley*. I close the
distance between Susan and me and she gives me a revolted
look like I am something disgusting that hitched a ride in
on the sole of her designer heels.

'Arrgh.' I roar. She looks like a stunned mullet as I whip
the stapler out from behind, unlock the pin so it opens and
squeeze down on the upper half. A staple exits and jams
into my finger. I stare at it momentarily. Well, that didn't
work as I thought it would. I had tried to conquer my
nerves and force myself into action, hoping to distract her
enough by imagining myself as an angered librarian firing
staples at the villain who would back away in disbelief. She
stares at my hand before I bring the bird out from behind
me with the opposite hand throwing over-hand as Gavin
had taught me before I am grabbed from behind, my arms
pinioned as the bird makes contact with my opponent's
face. Well, it did distract her, but not as I had imagined.

'You naughty thing.' Susan lifts the syringe and I grit my teeth as it plunges into my arm. 'Night night.'

Gavin

I grip my bat and spot S2 hurrying away with her thugs, Alara and the doctor thrown over the shoulders of a giant of a man. I follow close behind as they head to a van and scramble into the vehicle. As it slowly pulls out of the carpark I rush to Mr Aldidge's car and clamber into the driver's side. As the vehicle roars to life, the engine drops to a satisfying purr and I follow with the headlights switched off.

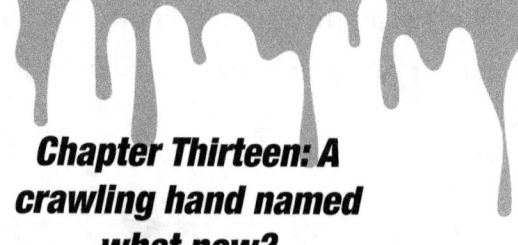

Chapter Thirteen: A crawling hand named what now?

Alara

I groan and clutch at my aching head; the insistent sound of dripping catches my attention and I open my eyes. I never thought in my wildest imaginings I would be fighting off evil corporations, zombies and defending kindly doctors while experiencing love and heartbreak. It is like something out of a horror or science fiction novel. And it is far from glamorous, unlike the epic stories I have read.

I scan the room; a single light bulb gives off dim yellowish light and reminds me of Gavin's new eyes. I bite my lip to stop it trembling and note the damp liquid sweating through the brown stone walls. The floor is packed earth and a weathered wooden staircase leads to a door. I pat the top of my head realising Gavin's hat is gone; tears prickle in my eyes like hot needles.

I climb the steps; my foot falls through and scrapes my bare ankle. I whistle through my teeth, trying to ignore the pain and withdraw my appendage. Picking out the splinters, I proceed cautiously up the stairs. I pause and take a deep breath; there has got to be traps. Why have they kept me alive?

I slide off a shoe and toss it at the door expecting it to be zapped or burnt to a crisp. I tap my foot impatiently, take a deep breath and exhale deeply before retrieving the shoe and replacing it on my foot. I search around the vicinity for any trip wires or anything out of place.

'Buzzzz.'

I jump as I nearly trip over a figure lying prone.

'You look like you might have to change your undies,' cackles an older man who groans and sits up. 'I've been here a while.' He smiles broadly. 'You find amusement where you can.' He whistles suddenly. A tin can rolls across the floor and lands at the base of the dilapidated stairs. 'Meet my good old mate, Fred. He was a top-notch bloke, always thinking of others.'

I back away as a disembodied green hand scurries up the steps like a loyal pet. My fellow prisoner tickles the back of the hand like he is stroking a dog. The hand waggles its fingers like it appreciates it.

'Fred loves this.'

'You have named it?' I squash my surprise and turn my attention back to the door and reach for the handle. To my surprise Fred, umm the hand, whatever, lands on the handle and clings to it like it has been flung. The hand writhes as if it is in pain before sliding and flopping about on the floor like a fish on land.

'Careful now or you will turn like my mate Fred did.'

I sit down and cross my legs. Fred twitches and scurries past me down the steps and crawls inside the tin can. I turn back to the older man as he continues his story.

'I ran during the first outbreak. Me and my mate, but he got bit. Tried to dispatch the injured hand and it turned into my mate down there and fled down a drainpipe. I was a coward and kept going, while, one hand less, Fred fought the others chasing me. But the hand was returned to me, like my friend was still with me. It landed in my hands as it was flung from some window. We've been together ever since.'

'How did you end up here?'

'I'm Ted by the way.' He reaches out his hand and I shake it.

'Alara.'

'I climbed the fence and tried rummaging through their bins for something to eat. Happened upon some shady stuff, knocked out, woke up here.'

I grind my teeth and stand before I stretch and hurry down the stairs to do something absurd. I bend down and pick up the can. Shuddering, I peer into it, the fingers wiggle like decomposing worms and I squash the urge to vomit. 'Ah, thanks for your help, Fred.'

I place the can back down on the ground and return to where Ted is. The door opens and Susan enters followed by armed personnel. She gestures towards Ted and an armed woman drags the older man through the doors.

'Nice meeting you, miss. Don't forget to recycle the can.'

I rush Susan and several guns are pointed at me. I back down the stairs and trip, my leg twists at an odd angle and I howl with pain. 'Kelley's dead. Her husband is loose and we need to deal with him. Give this one a spa treatment.' Susan turns on her heel and the others follow through the door and it slams shut behind them.

Warm water trickles down my legs and I groan; I hope I haven't soiled myself. I wince and shift my leg into a flat position, gritting my teeth as the pain floods through me. There is a scream in the hallway and I cover my ears. Water drips on my back and I turn. Frigid liquid seeps through the wall, cold mud squelches under me. I drag myself slowly backwards towards the steps with my hands, trying to mute my screams as the muddy water washes over my thighs. The can begins to float and I snatch it, tossing it by the door; it clanks as it rolls around. The sound of action reaches my ears as I reach the lower step and hoist myself up, my heart dully thudding in my chest as the cold murky water reaches my waist.

I scream as I reach the top of the stairs and lean against a wall, the water rises to my neck. Gunfire follows my yelling. And I sob as I stand on tiptoe, craning my chin upwards as the water line swells, the light reflected on its dark surface. I duck my head under water and notice a crack in the wall and push myself towards it before rushing to the surface for another breath; sweet air feels my struggling lungs.

Something crashes into the door. My sobs are muted as the water rushes over my head. I clutch at the wall and kick towards the surface with my good leg. I gasp, taking in a deep breath before the room is completely flooded. Between the ceiling and the body of water, is a small gap. I swim, but I can't reach that air pocket despite lodging my good leg in the crack and pushing myself upwards.

My skin crawls as warm flesh brushes my hand and I stiffen; fingers pry my clenched fist apart and shove something into my grip.

I feel the object with my other hand, two openings, some kind of hollow object. In one last desperate burst, I surge upwards, pushing off the wall with one foot to give me anchorage I thrust the tube in my mouth and hold the other end up and breathe.

Air rushes into my lungs and, to save it, I turn my head back towards the water and exhale, making sure the tube doesn't touch it.

Gavin

My body aches with the urge to give myself over to the rage and hunger flooding my body like venom. Those who harmed them must all die and I will consume their brains for what they did to Kelley, Grace and Alara.

I take a deep breath and glance about at the landscape of freshly laid concrete and tin sheds as far as the eye can see. I have only been here once and this all looks fairly new. Where is she being kept? I have to decide fast. Who knows what they are doing to my sweet wife?

I pace back and forth, my hands tightly gripping the handle of the cricket bat, before I hurry down the side of a silver shed, turn and try the handle of a green one. Of course it's locked. Exhaustion sweeps over me in a tedious wave and I lean against another shed and slide down its surface to sit on the ground, my back leaning into it.

This is pointless I won't find her. My vision alights on a misshapen object and my heart beats furiously with renewed vigour. I lean forward and snatch up my discarded lucky hat. Facing me is a blue shed; light peaks out from under the door. I scramble to my feet just as the handle turns and a security guard runs screaming past me. A horde of zombies rushes towards me and I lift my bat.

Alara

I never imagined I would drown alone in a room during a zombie apocalypse. He won't find me. Surely I should just give in to the cold, wet darkness.

'Alara.' Gavin pounds against the door. 'Grrr ... are ... brains ... you ... delicious ... alive?'

That voice. He's come for me.

'Where are you?'

I can not answer as I concentrate on breathing. I quell the urge to cry, saving my energy, and continue to regulate my breathing. I suppress the urge to wriggle as the hand, I mean Fred, uses my legs to pull itself downwards. With my next breath I feel dizzy, noting there isn't enough air to sustain me for long.

I close my eyes to the accompaniment of the pounding on the door. My first kiss flashes past, my dad teaching me to read and propagating my love of books, my mother's gentle words as she nursed a grazed knee from some bush-walk she took me on.

'I love you, Alara. Answer me ... grr.'

As my energy fades those words comfort me as my leg cramps and gives way. The water level drops miraculously and fast; a large gurgle develops into a roar and I fall on to the upper deck. A horrid groan mixed with a scream unleashes itself from my mouth. The steel door looks like it had been beaten from the outside.

Gavin's sobs can be heard on the other side. 'Love, answer me.'

'Get me out of here.'

The door crashes open and there stands my love covered in gore, his lucky hat torn to shreds, a cricket bat split in half and clutched in his bleeding hands. And he's never looked more brilliant.

He drops the bat, his eyes red from crying and still shiny with new unshed tears, and slams to his knees in front of me and lifts me into his arms. His mouth finds mine and my heart stops before it beats again as his strength and warmth spreads throughout my injured body. 'Kelley is dead and my bat is broken. But she would have bloody approved of it breaking to try and save you.'

'I'll replace it,' I force out.

He shakes his head. 'No, that chapter is closed and re-placing it would only lessen the sacrifice.' He stands with me in his arms and hurries through the door and turns my head into his chest. 'Not for the likes of you to see such violence. You are too innocent; your wild gentle imagina-tion can't be lost to this.'

We exit the building and I lift my head; flashing lights from emergency vehicles assault my senses. The light from a reporter's camera pushed in my face causes me to blink rapidly and a cacophony of voices makes my ears ache.

An ambo steps forward and points to the stretcher, Gavin growls and lowers me on to it before stepping back-wards. I am wrapped in a blanket as my love turns his back on me to answer some questions. A hot beverage is placed in my hands which shake from the cold.

A police officer sounds his siren and startles the reporter. 'Get out of here, you scoundrels. The people we've rescued from the experiments need space.'

As the noise drifts away I am loaded into the back of the ambulance. 'Gavin, I need Gavin,' I shout to his retreating back.

He pauses and hurries back and places his lucky hat on my head. 'It must be lucky. I found you tonight and I am sure one day it will lead me back to you. One day, when I can be assured I can't hurt you, we will be together.' My gallant knight, my lover, my gentle farmer, turns on his heel, his shoulders slump as he hurries over to a nurse and she escorts him out of my sight.

Different tropes for different folks

As is the quirky nature of Ima Ghoul, she has turned the tables and offered the reader one of two choices ... don't worry they are both HEAs. Alara deserves that and so does our reader, as I am sure you have preferred tropes. So, those who prefer no pregnancy and kid-related tropes in their happily ever after, avoid alternate ending two and epilogue two. Enjoy!

Alternate Ending One:
Every dog has her day,
even a zombie one

One year later: Gavin

My stomach plummets as I wander through the ruins of my once grouse little town. After I had been admitted to the hospital, in between treatments I had watched the world full apart on the telly. New plagues flooded the world taking lives and eventually the hospital was all but abandoned except for Doctor Dalage, his wife and a few other specialists. I had relayed Kelley's final message to the doctor I now considered a friend who had taken her body to the lab and I hadn't seen him in nearly a week. Then I had been given so-called medicine; foul tasting liquids that burned the mouth. Strewth, it had hurt. But it dulled the cravings and I continued to take them in hopes of a cure.

I wander down Alara's street. Her house has long since been ransacked but I often patrol the library hoping to catch her, chasing off looting blighters in case she ever returned. The last I'd heard she had been transferred to a private facility for specialist care in her nan's town. Two days later the lines went down and the town was overrun, all played out before us on the television. I had wanted to leave and go find Alara but the doctor had assured me the last phone call he'd had he was told that citizens in the facilities had been evacuated, but he didn't know where. That night I had thrown beer cans at the telly and gotten drunk.

It's now her birthday and a year later. I stall outside Mr Aldridge's door before I knock. I've tried this on several occasions with no luck.

'Yes.'

Bloody heck, he's alive. 'Mr Aldridge, it's me Gavin Smith.'

The door opens and his little dog scampers around my feet.

An older zombie woman rushes me, dressed in an ancient nighty, a rolling pin in her hand, flour streaking her face. 'Be gone or I'll do you in like Chester.'

I bolt. I can't do this; I am just retracing old wounds. Scamp rushes past me, barking between bouts of strange growls. I halt when I can no longer run; the breath rushes out of me in a hot gush and I bend over, my lungs heaving with the effort from my rushed exertions. The dog begins digging at a fresh patch of dirt amongst withering flowers near the library doors.

Scamp dislodges something. I pick it up and shake it free of its earthy crust. My hands twitch as I clutch the tattered remnants of my lucky hat and I turn to face the bordered-up doors. The glass had shattered and I had covered it with rough planks of wood, I had needed to keep busy. She's been here, the board has been pushed away and I hurry inside. There, with her back turned placing a new hat on her old desk, is my wife.

I don't think, I hurry towards her and turn her to face me and crush her into my arms before our mouths meet in a long, drawn out kiss.

The little dog bounces excitedly around our feet and I pull away breathless. Tears run down her face and I kiss them away.

She pulls back to smile up at me. 'I found my way back to you.'

'You will have to tell me all about it. I snatch her hand in mine afraid she is some spook here to torment me, but her hand is warm flesh beneath my own and there will be even more when I get her back to the farm.

I reach down and pat the dog. 'You did good, Scamp, every dog has her day, mate, even zombie ones.'

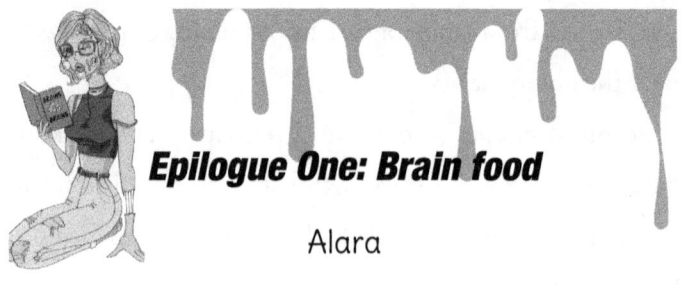

Epilogue One: Brain food

Alara

My happily ever after is surreal. With Scamp bounding at my heels we hurry back to the car parked on the side of the road. Gavin grips my hand, my fingers throb but I am so glad to have found him I ignore the intense pressure. He opens my door; as I slide into the front passenger side he finally releases my hand, his eyes locked on mine until he slams the door. I smile as he has grown back the mullet he is fond of.

Hurrying around to the other side, he bends down and picks up Scamp. Opening his side, he gently passes the little dog across to me before settling into the driver's seat and closing his door. Sliding the key into the ignition the car roars to life.

'We need to look for Mr Aldridge.'

I nod and the car pulls away from the curb, and with a click he puts on his seatbelt. We cruise around town, disco music playing from the 8 track; Gavin drums his keys in time with the song, his gaze scanning the area for our friend.

'So. It's been a year.'

'Yeah.'

He breaks suddenly, his breathing quickens and he turns in his seat. 'I thought ... you were de—'

I lean over, placing my hand over his mouth, and he begins mouthing my fingers. His jagged teeth nip at my skin, the sensation is enticing as it is unnerving.

'The area surrounding the city was overcome with zombies. Military officers evacuated us in waves. Zombies, even non-feral ones were overlooked.' I smile. 'But Susan and her board were found guilty and transported to a remaining military based for long-term holding.'

'Good news at least.' His gaze intensifies. 'How did you get out?'

I grimace. 'It wasn't pleasant. Hitched a ride amongst some zombie sheep being transported to the new base. Then after eleven months of treatment they decided I wasn't going to go feral and released me. It took me weeks of petitioning the higherups to get someone to take me back here. I arrived near dawn.'

He snatches my hand and frowns. 'Why didn't you go back to the farm?'

Tears form in my eyes. 'I did this morning and couldn't find you. I took your rusty bicycle out of the shed, gave it a wipe down and cycled here; I will feel it later. when I couldn't get a hold of my neighbour and saw my house ransacked I assumed you may have been dead.'

I sniffle as tears slide down my cheeks. 'I acquired a new hat for you in case I found you.'

He brushes a lock of hair out of my eyes and presses a gentle kiss to each part my tears marked. 'It's like you gave it a funeral, burying your grief. You sappy woman. Blimey I love you.'

Scamp begins to whine and leaps out of the window. I am rather indisposed as Gavin leans in, tracing kisses across my collarbone, unbuttoning the top button of my blouse.

The dog howls, a startling sound between a moan and a yap. Gavin bolts upright, wincing as his head hits the roof. 'Strewth.'

My cheeks heat and I slide down in the seat as Mr Aldridge grins at me. 'Good to see a wedded couple still blissfully happy.' My neighbour hands me an envelope.

'We didn't find you at yours, mate. Was worried for you.' Gavin takes the envelope, opening it while I button my blouse, before he gawps at the contents then suddenly grins. 'It's official. You are my lawfully wedded wife.

My brows furrow. 'How? There are no major governing bodies.'

'Tell Pat that.' Mr Aldridge claps his hands together. 'Our Mayor is still holding parliament. Sharon who still works in the post office and is a Justice of the Peace witnessed it and delivered it back to me yesterday. The remaining residents communicate with flyers and letters. Pat also recognised Kelley Smith's prior death certificate.'

I glance at Gavin, a fleeting look of sadness in his eyes, before he squeezes my hand. 'I'm alright.'

My old neighbour reaches into the jacket of his coat. 'Had to keep her warm. I got a present for you, quite chilly this evening despite being spring. Mary mentioned you'd been around, Gavin.'

My heart skips a beat and he withdraws a shivering, tiny green pup.

'Scamp had pups. This is the last to find a home.'

'Oh, she's perfect.' I clutch the pup to my chest.

As I coo over the little ball of floof Gavin frowns. 'There's an angry woman in your house. She says she did something to a Chester.'

Mr Aldridge chuckles. 'That's Mary, my new sheila, we had a row. She kicked me out for a stroll, she has a temper.'

I scratch the pup behind her ears. 'Chester is Mr Aldridge's first name.'

Gavin laughs. 'Alright, mate. Do you have enough tucker?'

'Plenty, freezer's full. Oh.' He almost leaps in through the window with excitement. 'That doctor friend of yours reckons he's really close to a cure. Days he said.'

My husband's eyes almost bug out of his head and he grips the steering wheel. 'We will go to Dalage's now.'

My former neighbour waves us off and the car pulls away, slowing into the next street as Gavin parks the car.

I wring my hands while kneeling by my groaning husband who has collapsed on the white tiled floor. I glance around; shelves line the walls stocked with shelf-stable medicines. I glance at Gavin and he sits up, staring at his hand. As his eyes lock on mine, I gasp. 'They are back to their old colour.'

'That was awful.' He frowns. 'What was worse, seeing you go through it first.'

'Equally as bad seeing you do it too.' I stroke the dog whining by my feet, and my eyes lock on the doctor as he leans down to pat the animal. 'Not the pup. Don't give any to her.'

'Would never do that to an unaware pooch.' The puppy whines and wags her tail. 'Plus, I only had enough full doses for three or four people. You two, Mary and Chester. The rest will be used to develop a cure for more people.'

'Thanks doc.' Gavin stands and holds out his hand to the doctor who shakes it. 'What was it made from?'

The doctor winces. 'That information was between Kelley and myself.'

Gavin's face becomes ashen. 'You made something from her.' He turns to me and tears well in his eyes. 'I reckon her body had the cure like some kind of brain food.'

Dr Dalage holds open the door. 'Sorry guys, I must ask you to leave, other people to see, of course.'

As I retrieve my pet, Gavin snatches my other hand and hurries through the door.

'Gavin, are you alright?'

'I will be, can't believe I had to say bye again and now this cure is from her remains. If only there was some way to remember her by. It's like all her good work will be forgotten.'

The pain in his voice grips my heart like it is clutched in a zombie's supernatural grip. I reach out and touch his shoulder as my pup barks. 'Can I name the pup Kel?'

My husband turns me into his arms. 'That would be grouse.'

He smiles sadly and pulls away, petting the dog gently before he looks at me. 'Do you hate cricket?'

I raise a brow. 'I am learning all the time, but no, I love it.'

He smiles as if I have conquered the world for him; the truth is we did it for each other.

'Oh wait.' He pulls a crinkled five dollar note from his pocket and hands it to me. 'Should have given it to you for your last birthday.'

I extend my hand and pocket the note, and smile. 'Strewth, I love you,' I mutter.

As he kisses me, the pup snuggles against my chest. I ponder of how I came to this moment, to this contentment.

I'm Alara Smith, a thirty-five-year-old librarian from a small country town in South Australia. Two years ago, I hadn't been kissed, now I have a hubby, a pup and a weird and wacky but exciting future ahead of me. Who would have thought zombies and cricket would bring me happiness? Kel barks, I guess she agrees.

Gavin

The sweat beads on my brow and my eyes lock on the batswoman before me. I dip my cap to the bowler, now a zombie.

'Brrr ... ains.' William our ex-coach mutters and raises his arm to throw, blimey, he can still bowl.

Alara tenses and I guide my hands over hers, our newest teammate. As the ball hurtles towards her, my arms guide her swing. With a thunderous crack the ball flies away from us.

'Strewth. Well done, love.' Her eyes glisten with excitement and I remove my cap and lean in to kiss her.

'Run ... grrr.' David half-shuffles half-runs towards us and I pat Alara on her rump. With a giggle, she bolts to the other side of the pitch and David steps into her former spot.

I'm Gavin, a forty-four-year-old sheep farmer from a small town in South Australia. Who would have thought I'd gain a wife, a dog and still be able to play cricket, especially with my girl, during a zombie apocalypse? I reckon it turned out alright.

The End.

Alternate Ending Two:
Brain smoothie

Alara

After my terrible bouts of nausea for the last two days, my stomach had begun to swell and take on a strange emerald hue and I had almost passed out until Gavin had me admitted to hospital. On a positive note, it's been three weeks since my rescue and we received our official statement of marriage yesterday, the authorities-that-be recognising the prior and new death certificate. I had celebrated with a salad and a massage; after watching Gavin chow down on his meal I couldn't stomach anything else.

The technician running the probe over my abdomen gives me a sad smile before she turns the screen to Dr Dalage. I'm seeing twenty weeks along at least.'

The doctor's brows knit together. 'With everything that's going on I wouldn't put it past a rapid pregnancy.'

Gavin scoffs, his lucky hat clutched between both hands, before his cheeks bloom with a delicate pink. His gaze lowers to his boots. 'We weren't proper careful about three months ago and ah, recently.'

My eyes widen and I assume my cheeks match my husband's. 'Don't say that, they will know stuff. Bedroom stuff.'

Gavin guffaws loudly. 'They probably assume as much with a kid in you.'

The technician jumps and shakes her head. 'Mr Smith, this is a hospital.'

Gavin smiles. 'Sorry, miss.'

Dr Dalage steps towards us and sighs. 'We've seen this in other pregnant women after activities of a romantic nature with a zombie partner. The foetus develops rapidly and begins to turn the mother and we lose both of them by the fifth day. But I may have a solution.'

Gavin slams his hat on his head. 'Anything to save Alara.'

The doctor's brows furrow. I will try to save both your wife and your daughter. But Alara will have to do something dreadful.'

Gavin shoves his hands in the pocket of his jeans. 'Is it what I had to do?'

Dr Dalage nods and turns his gaze to me. 'You will have to consume the brains of Kelley to prevent the spread of infection throughout your body, and hopefully your foetus won't use its chompers to gain entry into the world.'

'I won't. Nothing ...'—my words falter—'will make me change my mind.' I slide off the bed and run, my bare feet slapping on the speckled grey linoleum, the cream walls rushing past as I refuse to believe this is happening. I am reading some ludicrous novel and have become too absorbed in its pages.

'Alara Smith!'

The sound of heavy boots and the desperation in that voice causes me to halt. A warm body slams into me from behind, his ragged breath on the back of my neck as his leans down to place his cheek against mine, thick strong muscular arms wrapping around my thickening belly protectively.

I try to wrench myself away but he locks me against his torso. 'Don't do this. You have to live.'

He loosens his grasp and I turn in his arms; my mouth forms a wide O, his eyes are no longer yellow.

'Did you do it?' I gulp.

He nods and he looses a long, ragged breath. 'Yes and she was my ... we were a family once.' He lets out a pitiful groan as he pulls away and covers his face with his hands, muted sobs rack his frame. 'I can't lose you, Alara. Kelley was bad enough, Gracie was almost the death of me. But you ... and now this baby are my hope that humanity can get through this chaotic snippet in its long, enduring story.'

I blink in surprise at his almost poetic account of the apocalypse. If he can do it, this kind, gentle man, so can I. 'Let's get it over with.'

Gavin takes my hand and hurries me back to the sparse hospital room I had fled. He takes off his coat and I walk into its warmth, earthy just like his stoicism as he protects my dignity. 'Your gown came undone.'

I take a deep breath and enter the room. The technician has left and Gavin closes the door behind me and stands against it, his arms crossed as the doctor pulls a vial from his pocket.

'This vial contains trace amounts of the powdered umm, main ingredient, and a blood stabiliser. It is painful and survival isn't guaranteed.'

My pulse quickens. 'My odds without it?'

Dr Dalage frowns. 'Nil.'

I swallow hard and reach for the vial, unstopper it and swill the contents. It tastes like sand, the grit sticking to my tongue like an abrasive coating before the pain starts, filling my chest with lancing needles. As I feel myself falling, firm hands sweep me up into those muscular arms. 'I've got both my girls safe.'

Epilogue Two: Green is still my favourite colour

Two months later: Alara

G avin tilts his head at me and blinks rapidly. 'You want to call her what?'

'Chrysoberyl Grace. Green gemstones represent new beginnings.' I close the book titled Gemology For Newbies and add it to the pile on the overbed table weighed down with others I had Gavin check out for me. I have been bedridden these last few months, Dr Dalage too afraid to let me and bubs out of his gentle medical supervision. I sigh and a wave of contentment settles my shaky nerves. 'And after—'

My husband's gaze softens. 'After Grace and ... Beryl was Kelley's middle name. Did I mention that?' He laughs. 'Did you comb through books seeking that exact thing?'

'Maybe.' I smile. 'We can call her Chrys for short. You mentioned the middle name thing once. I think.'

My husband lowers a hand towards the green-skinned infant, her cat-like pale yellow eyes flitter about seeking his;

like most newborns her eyesight is unfocused. A tiny hand wraps around his pinkie. 'I'm glad she's alright with the rapid pregnancy thing.'

As my husband coos to his new baby there is a knock and Dr Dalage enters with a clipboard, a huge smile on his face. 'I won't stay long, but good news.' He turns and closes over the door. 'Alara will make a full recovery.' He sighs as he stares at the glass cot. 'The baby isn't free of it. You will have to add powdered brains to her bottles. Hopefully down the track we can find a cure for those born with the virus too.'

Gavin turns and shakes hands with the doctor. 'So, Alara will be fine?'

'I can't say the same for you, Gavin. You aren't prone to aggression anymore and your eyes have returned to their original form, but it seems the cure doesn't work for every-one.' The doctor sighs. 'Well, I have lots to do and still have to notify the media that we are on our way to a cure.'

As Gavin shows our friend out, I reach for my daughter. 'Ah baby girl. We will get through this strange new chapter in humanity's life together. Mummy and daddy are here darling and green is still my favourite colour.'

While it took a zombie apocalypse to give me inspira-tion to live life to the full, I am grateful. I am Alara, a thirty-four-year-old librarian who has been kissed, landed a hubby and a bub all while helping save the library.

Gavin

The sweat beads on my brow and my eyes lock on the batswoman before me. I dip my cap to the bowler, now a zombie.

'Brrr ... ains.' William our ex-coach mutters and raises his arm to throw, blimey, he can still bowl.

Alara tenses and I guide my hands over hers, our newest teammate; as the ball hurtles towards her, my arms guide her swing. With a thunderous crack the ball flies away from us.

'Strewth. Well done, love ... grrr.' Her eyes glisten with excitement and I remove my cap and lean in to kiss her.

'Run ... tasty brains.' David half-shuffles half-runs towards us, calling out my wife's nickname given to her by our teammates and I pat Alara on her rump. With a giggle, she bolts to the other side of the pitch and David steps into her former spot.

I'm Gavin, a forty-three-year-old sheep farmer from a small town in South Australia. Who would have thought I'd gain a wife, a kid and still be able to play cricket, especially with my girl, during a zombie apocalypse? I reckon it turned out alright even if I am a little green around the gills.

The End.

Acknowledgements

I would like to thank my amazing editor Jenn Zabinskas from RedInk Creative, who puts up with my [1]vommenting in DMs when my quirky brain forms new ideas. Her professionalism and staunch support encourages me to continue to write.

Also, to my dedicated readers, especially to Meagan Maslen, thank you, there wouldn't be this sequel without you. Also a thank you to Dani and your tips on cricket, much appreciated.

[1] When a person comments on a post or in a DM so fast it is like it was blurted out and may contain spelling errors or other inaccuracies in the areas of grammar or punctuation.

---

1. When a person comments on a post or in a DM so fast it is like it was blurted out and may contain spelling errors or other inaccuracies in the areas of grammar or punctuation.

About the author

Ima Ghoul enjoys breaking confines, offering stories that encourage the reader to interact, and writes quirky short stories full of hilarity and heart. Able to write across multiple genres, Ima has put her pen to works in sci-fi, mild horror, fantasy and closed-door romances.

Ima first knew she wanted to be a writer when she would make up bold games as a child and enact them out with her siblings. She enjoys long walks amongst ancient trees as it is grounding to her wild soul, and loves archery and role playing games. Her home is a place of organised chaos with three children, a hubby and five chickens as she adores animals, especially birds and deer.

Ima once had a fascination for pig latin and her love of deer lead to her gamer tag AwnFay. This new interest encouraged her to create her own languages as a kid and plays a big part in her fantasy writing under her other pen name. An avid reader first, Ima devours tomes in a day then spends hours reminiscing over them.

Her first novella Zombies & Papercuts started out as a fun little activity and feedback from a reader encouraged her to write a sequel. This has lead to her writing more short stories and closed-door romances which she has found she has a knack for and hopes to share her joy for writing them with her readers.

Also by Ima Ghoul

Zombies & Papercuts

Would you believe it I am Would you believe it I am thirty-three and have never been pashed? Let me introduce myself, my name is Alara and I am a librarian in a small country town in South Australia and a local nobody. As my luck would have it, doom coincides with my birthday and the party guests happen to be zombies.

But I am an eternal optimist. Will today be the day I finally share my first kiss? Armed only with my wit and books let's hope I don't get a papercut. They hurt more than a zombie bite.

Weird & Wacky Anthology: Volume One

Delve into the the wacky, the witty and mildly creepy, from tales of magic, aliens and ghouls to sweet romances.

Ima Ghoul, author of Zombies and Papercuts, brings the adventurous reader an anthology of short stories that won't fail to tantalise and amuse.

Will you cross the threshold?

Turn the page ... I dare you!

Zombies & Cricket

The night fills with the familiar chirp of crickets and the irritating hum of mozzies. I swat at one. My chest tightens as I lick my lips, trying to will away the intrusive thought, and now guilty pleasure, of wondering if mozzies have edible brains. So, it is happening, and relatively fast.

After the zombie apocalypse, the government found a temporary solution and encouraged us to continue living our lives. Let me introduce myself. My name is Gavin, a 43-year-old cattle farmer from South Australia, with a love of cricket. As the one—year anniversary—now aptly named Use Your Noggin Day—and my gal's birthday, approaches, there has been an increase in zombie attacks.

Will I be able to protect Alara, keep my humanity and still play the match next weekend?